THE MONKEY KING

NICK PHILLIOU

ISBN: 069253914X
ISBN 13: 9780692539149

I dedicate this book to my family.

Prologue
INDIA

My mom says that I entered the world along with millions of different bright colors and sweet smells. It was almost thirteen years ago in a remote part of the Himalayan Mountains known as the Valley of Flowers where my own dad delivered me. The village we stayed in was so isolated that I was even allowed to go outside and to be seen in public. Those were probably the only six months of my life not lived in fear.

The few people who knew about me seemed to think I was special and brought me gifts. My parents named me after one of their gods in fact, Hanuman.

Life in the Valley of Flowers was probably pretty peaceful, until the night it all ended. It was the last physical contact my mother and I had with my father.

They had come for us in the cover of darkness on a moonless night. One of dad's doctor friends knew they were coming and helped my mom and I escape. But the ones who put a black bag over my father's head and tied his hands behind his back got what they wanted.

We were smuggled by ambulance and then flown on a small plane to the United States. We landed in Newark Airport, and I haven't left New Jersey since.

Chapter 1
WANT AD

Crisp air and neon light were welcome when the doors finally sucked themselves open. The stale, flannel covered atmosphere of the bus had become claustrophobic.

Only five or six weak kneed caffeine addicts followed behind him. It was nearing the end of February, and many looked miserable because of the cold. The fighter let them pass. He moved himself away from the mechanical glow to stand beneath a canopy of shimmering stars.

He rummaged through his pockets and separated trash from anything important. The bus inhaled, then tiredly wheezed. It coughed out sharply to shut down and settled in for a refill.

The fighter put his hands in his pockets, glad to be out of the vacuous, rolling tube. He stood still and watched a hundred heavenly bodies in the distance.

The night sky seemed so vast and free to him. He tried to deny being already homesick. After all it had been less than twenty-four hours since he last hugged Lenora, boarded the bus, and left the mountain town he had grown up in.

The bus revived itself more quickly than he had hoped. It sounded as if it was being resuscitated from death when it vacuumed in cold air from the crystalline night.

Before re-boarding he decided to look at the job-ad one more time. Lenora had printed a thorough poop-sheet for him, in case he lost his phone or smashed it again in an un-medicated explosive fit of rage.

The paper felt alive in his hand, like a butterfly in torpor. It read:

Personal Martial Arts Coach

We are looking for a one on one coach for our special home-schooled twelve year old. This is a full time job with guest room available. Must be very well versed in several martial arts. (Please list all tournament records, MMA titles held, and awards received.) Must have experience with exceptional learner adolescents. (Teaching certificate is helpful but not required). Background check. Confidentiality agreement. Contract. State of the art training facilities provided. High figure salary. Will provide transportation fees for face-to-face interview.
CONTACT: Babazukes@goodforyou.com

"High figure salary..." comes out of his mouth in a cloud of frozen air. He's reminded that he not only had to forfeit his last fight's prize money, but had to pay hefty fines as well.

The words, "Exceptional learner," were drowned out by the bus's huffs and puffs.

———

At five in the morning and in the dead of Winter Alpine New Jersey was frigid. Forty feet up a tree, with wind blowing in from the north someone from New Jersey might even say that it was freaking freezing!

Han wore his own insulation, stuff he modeled off of Navy SEAL winter-ops gear. The homemade long johns fit snuggly underneath supple and soft rip-stop. His 3-D printed jeans and sweatshirt were designed from Ambercrombie and Fitch's back-to-school line. His feet and hands remained bare, while his head stayed warm within the protection of a thermal regulated ski mask.

"The stars, especially at this hour, have a tough time competing with New York's lights," he spoke softly into his phone. "I hope that I get to see the stars how they're supposed to be seen." Han's hearing stretched outward when he closed his eyes. Route 9W, the highway leading towards the George Washington Bridge and the bright illumination of New York City whirred with 100 mph auto-piloted taxi cabs and glowed with the light trails left behind from even faster sensor protected motorcycles.

"It's freezing up here but I can't sleep inside, not tonight," he said as his eyes reopened. Han's pupils dilated when they met the light from his phone. "Aeson's coming in today for his interview and I hope he likes me. He won't be afraid of me at least. Grandpa says this guy's, *not afraid of nothing.* That's how I want to be, fearless."

Han's lanky strong frame curled up in the armpit of several thick oak limbs. What was left of the stars began to fade. Before he slept completely, and the not too distant highway became the background sound for his dreams, he reached for a thin ultra-warm solar blanket that he stashed earlier in a branch. It had soaked up a day's worth of thermal energy. An abandoned squirrel nest, packed with layers of soft leaves became his loamy pillow. Before shutting his phone off he made a final digital diary entry then wrote a brief text to Aeson Cadmus. Han wished him a safe journey on his way to the interview.

———

Before he settled back into his seat Aeson watched others squirm and shift, wrap themselves in blankets, and hug pillows to get comfortable.

The kids across from him leaned against each other with closed eyes. He wondered if they were fake-sleeping and suspected they would wake as soon as the rest of the passengers started snoring again. He tucked Lenora's emergency data points back into his pocket, folded his arms, and leaned into the corner for another uncomfortable nap.

Dreams took the fighter immediately. He crushed a giant ogre-like opponent's nose in the arena of his subconscious. He used a leaping super-man punch. A spray of blood caused him to blink.

He awakened to the sounds of cheering fans.

They're not rooting for me. They'll never root for me again... he groggily convinced himself.

———

"Hey kid! It's freezing out here!" Han's uncle Al screamed up the tree. Alfonso Zucharino held his phone in his hand. Having dialed Han for thirty minutes without reward he clutched the device as if it were something useless, even burdensome.

Han continued to hug himself in sleep as his knees curled towards his face. His dream self stood on a battlefield as his own eyes moved rapidly back and forth under their lids.

Uncle Al circled the tree. The big man breathed out thick billows of mist. He was cold despite his purple cotton bath robe and the thick wool padded slippers that he wore. "Your mother's going to find out kid!" Al bellowed with a shiver.

Sun beams crisscrossed over Al's feet and he contemplated going back inside and having his coffee, making breakfast, and reading the fight columns in the several sports sites he subscribed to.

Han heard Katya scream his name. His on-line classmate only known through email, avatar, and most recently, texting, called for help from the barred window of a tall metal dream tower. Fires burned the base of the castle-like prison, and the flickering light began to blind Han's eyes. "I'm coming for you Katya!"

"What you saying?" Al asked the air as he turned back around to face the mighty oak again. "You screaming for that girl kid?"

The light was too strong to stare into. In his dream Han closed his eyes and turned from the flames and away from his potentially foolish

4

but heroic rescue attempt. In the waking world he opened his eyes and squinted. He regretted not saving Katya immediately but smiled in the warmth of the morning's first sun. His response to his uncle's plea came encased in cold mist as it exited his masked face, "Can you make kiwi pancakes please, Uncle Al!"

————

Darkness surrounded Aeson. He rubbed his eyes awake.

The fighter exhaled stress and inhaled relief as they taught him to do at the clinic.

Snores, whispered conversations, and soft electronic hums helped to remind him of where he actually was. A glow revealed a baggage shelf. Crayon colored knapsacks rested in a funnel of faint, dust filled light. The two little kids focused on a handheld screen. One was a boy, the other a girl. Their faces were cast in a moon-green glow.

The fighter imagined them both at first glance as insects; mischievously engaged, highly intelligent insects. The children actually thought the long ride was fun. With such huge seats to lay down in and stand up on, it felt practically like a camping trip.

"Use your jab, jab, jab! Superman Punch now!" shouted the little boy.

"Quiet Jai! There are people sleeping," announced a maternal voice from the seat behind them.

"Sorry ammi..." apologized the giggly pig-tailed sister who Jai was so enthusiastically coaching.

The fighter became more alert.

The early hour was sacred.

He stretched his spine and scanned the interior of the bus.

Passengers had sunk into their deep chairs and collapsed into contorted half-conscious positions. Aeson thought that many of them looked like insects. Others appeared to him as puppets. He worried that the medication the clinic put him on was making him a little crazy.

Other than the siblings who were happily engrossed in a game, the passengers made up a dreary orchestra that sounded like rusty saws and unchecked phlegm. The awakening fighter noticed how many seats glowed and had weird thoughts of alien probes hiding in dark fields.

Aeson touched the window. His fingers moistened with dew. He rubbed the water onto the back of his neck in an attempt to fully wake from the half-dream state. He wanted coffee, and knew he could get it at the next truck stop. He sat up but reclosed his eyes.

"Kimura!" the little girl yelled. "I have the Kimura!"

"Alisha! Where are your manners girl!" the mother demanded as she rose up in her seat.

"Break it Ali, break the goddamn arm!" was the excitedly unfiltered response of her brother, a six year old corner man.

Aeson's eyes opened fully, and an as of lately unfamiliar smile hatched across his face.

The mother of the two small children was tiny. She had to hang her short frame over the plaid throne-like bus seat to search for her swearing boy's head.

Her open palm slapped down on top of her son's neck as he bent for cover. The loud clap the hand made on the boy's skin caused Aeson to wince.

His smile retreated. He reached into his jacket pocket to find his phone and his prescription pills. The bottle went back in as he used his thumb to check messages. Two texts sat idly waiting to be read as he heard the kid squeal from his punishment.

I miss you Aeson. Are you still sure you want to do this? You don't have to. The East Coast is scary.

He read it over three times but only responded in his head:

Yes Lenora I'm sure I want to do this. Can't fight right now. And coaching will allow me to train. Scary? We'll see I guess.

The second message was from Han Zucharino; the kid he hoped to coach: **I hope you have a nice trip getting here Mr. Cadmus. We're all looking forward to meeting you.**

"Mr. Cadmus?" "We're all...?" Do I have the job or what? I thought I was only in the running. Rich kids, even if they are special, the fighter thought, should have to ride busses too. Only reason I didn't fly was to save some of the travel money.

The phone he read from began to vibrate in his hand.

He wiped away more dew and applied it to his face and head before answering.

"Hi babe. Wow, it's 5:00 in the morning back home and you're already awake? Just saw your text. Me, I'm probably in Pennsylvania by now. It's pitch black outside. Just trees, trees, and more trees. The kid, yeah, he's excited. Makes it sound like I already got the job."

Aeson wondered why she didn't say much. After all, she called him right?

"Hello. You there Lenora?"

"Yeah. I'm here. I'm glad your new student is psyched that's all."

"Good. I'm happy too," Aeson said, with "too" dropping off to become almost a whisper. There was more he wanted to tell her about his hopes, and about his concerns. "Coaching this kid is going to put me back on my path, I feel it."

"Are you saying I'm taking you off your PATH?" she asked sharply, which took Aeson by surprise and triggered him to search the pane for more spots of moisture. "After traveling with you to all those fights, hanging out in cheap hotels and smelly gyms, even sleeping in my car!" The fighter was pierced by her tone and held the phone away from his ear. He wondered, almost hoped, that she had been out all night at the bars, and that she was speaking from a drunken stupid place and not a sober vengeful one.

The new silence felt so massive that it created a shift in the fighter's mental awareness.

"No. You, you're part of my path," flopped out of him like a tired jab does just before the fight is lost. In that moment he hated the pills he was supposed to take. They made him feel too out of sorts and unable to respond intelligently to uncomfortable situations.

"I'm a little part of YOUR big plan! I thought martial-arts was about dropping your ego!"

Knockout delivered, for both parties. Suddenly it was time to say goodbye.

"I love you Aeson, you know that right?"

"I love you. I just don't have the words..."

"I know. Have a good day Aeson. Maybe call me when you get settled."

"You too. And yeah, I'll tell you all about it when I get there." With that he remembered the security and confidentiality contract he would have to sign before being hired. He wondered how much Lenora would be allowed to know about his new job.

The interstate seemed to go on forever. There was nothing but beetle eaten pine, road signs riddled with graffiti, bullet holes, and the corrosions of time.

He saw the Delaware River out the window and swore to himself in dawn's first light that he witnessed a bald eagle dive for its breakfast in the half frozen, slushy waters.

The bus refueled while Aeson bought a 32 ounce coffee. He sipped out of a cartoonishly large foam cup as the store's door opened and closed with weary travelers sliding their feet towards bathrooms, candy bars, and travel apps.

This might actually be the last truck-stop bean I drink for a while, he said to himself with a smile on his face and a feeling of sweet synthetic warmth cascading into his guts. If he hadn't checked his phone's history then his conversation with Lenora might have been dismissed as just a dream. No matter what was said though, he would be in New York, then New Jersey, and she'd be back home in the mountains of Southwest Colorado, two thousand miles away. It was time for him to do what he believed had to be done for his life to unfold.

The fluorescent lighting made the truck stop's bathroom emanate with a white, almost blinding quality. The alabaster tiles magnified the feeling of walking into the heart of a supernova. Pink liquid soap smelled like it looked, flowery and futuristic. Aeson tried to admire the contradictions;

the sunrise happening outside, the spaceship-like-room he was in, girly pink soap, and the knuckles of his own fists that nearly beat four men unconscious in the cage three weeks prior. He breathed in the laboratory aroma and threw water on his face, hair, and neck.

"Lend this guy a buck for a showah, c'mon dude, seriously," someone said, and continued to walk briskly out. It was a type of verbal mockery drive-by. The comment opened Aeson's wet eyes abruptly and allowed him to make visual contact with the third person in a moving party. The one he saw in the mirror wasn't the loud one, he could tell from his body language. The one he locked his eyes on was a slouched-shouldered crony who snickered at his boss's dumb jokes. He wore a TAPTHIS! shirt and was cultivating a strip of acne just below his scalded looking hair-line.

The hand dryer screamed like a crazed wind spirit and shot hot air into his still young but calloused face. Aeson's hair was growing back in a three week paramilitary fashion. He tried to like the new soft growth but couldn't really summon the need to care if his hair was long as a Rasta's or as bald as a Shaolin monk's. Aeson simply wanted to pound all three of those boys into oblivion and knew that if he hadn't taken those pills less than eight hours ago they'd already be bleeding.

He knew that, even groggy with anti-anger medication, if he let his mind set the world ablaze he'd run out to the parking lot and start swinging, kneeing, and body slamming. He retrieved his phone and stared at Lenora's number.

I can't call her now, not so soon after that last exchange. She could always calm the rage though. Lenora seemed to be the only non-pharmaceutical solution to an ever brewing Immediate Explosive Disorder moment.

He closed his eyes to imagine more vividly and tried to picture Lenora saying, "They're kids one-upping each other with how many tough looking guys they can put down without getting beaten up. It's not worth it Aeson. You're a trained fighter, a professional, not a thug brawler. Don't you want it all back? Don't you want me back?" In his daydream her green eyes glistened and made him wonder if he was making a mistake.

The crazed scream of the bathroom's hand dryer suddenly resumed. When the air finally stopped firing his eyes remained closed. The empty room was far from silent. Drips, light bulb buzz, a flushing toilet, and his own rapid breathing made for a chaotic concert. He noticed that his hands were wet again. Sweat coated his palms. He rinsed them, this time drying off on his jeans, in a hurry to leave and not waste a moment over-thinking things.

———

Han's other uncle, Salvatore, greeted him as he slunk in half asleep, "Breakfast's in the cave kid, let's go over the plan."

"Cool, yeah, play *Donnybrook* with me later, Uncle Sal."

"Sure kid, maybe after breakfast. You and me, *Donnybrook*, I love that game. Al! Let's go, kid's hungry! And he wants to fight!" Sal shouted as he faked an uppercut to Han's midsection.

"Keep it down you gavoon, I'm two feet in front of you and my ears work fine. Bring Pop his smoothy," Uncle Al replied while skillfully cracking an egg into a pan with one hand and attempting a handoff to his brother of a large glass of just pulverized vegetables.

"I ain't bringing him the smoothie before he has his espresso."

"Fine! Bring him the espresso!" Al finally snapped.

"Hey, keep it down guy, the kid's sleep walking," Uncle Sal retorted, suddenly taking on the role of mature adult.

Han closed his eyes, still wearing his cold weather mask, and let his arms go zombie. His blanket hung on top of his hands in an attempt to appear more ghostly.

"Look what you did now Sal, kid's really sleepwalking," said the smiling chef, making sure to finish his brotherly banter with kindness. He was always aware, thanks to his sister's sometimes stern reminders, of his nephew's formative emotions.

Han left his uncles to prepare the morning feast. He walked on tip-toes with his phone in his hand. He opened a door and was silent atop the thick, lush, red carpet of the steps that finished in the re-done basement. The staircase and its walls were designed to buffer sound. As far as noise was concerned all that went on in the basement area stayed in the basement.

The stairs entered into the main hang-out room, which, at first glance seemed like a sports bar and arcade in one. The main room lead to a gym, big and high tech enough to accommodate Olympic level athletes. A sliding glass door opened to Han's home school computer and scientific studies lab. Uncles Al and Sal both had private offices. Grandpa Vincent had his own woodshop that connected directly to a six car garage. Stella, Han's mother, had a yoga studio separate from the gym, but it was upstairs, to catch the first morning's light, and Han's grandmother had her own knitting room, also upstairs, where she looked out the window and watched birds skim bugs off the top of the pool in the humid afternoons of summer.

Han paused at the last step and stared into the softly lit space. His eyes tunneled in on the napping form and as he got closer the sound of snoring became louder. He sucked in his laughter and froze on one shaky foot. Han had to hide his eyes from the source of the snoring or else he'd really lose it.

Composing himself in a hunched over stalking stance Han began to whisper, "Morning Grandpa."

"Mmmmm."

"Uncle Sal said we're going to have a meeting or something."

"Mmmmm."

"Is now O.K?"

The first movements were from his hands. They were the biggest hands in the family, and the largest Han had has ever seen.

Patches of dark hair created small islands beneath and above bulbous knuckles. Han started to think that the hands before him had done a lot of physical work, and probably won a lot of tough fights.

The palms mounted themselves slowly onto the armrests of the large comfortable chair. Grandpa Vincent straightened, pushed backwards, and opened his eyes.

"Espresso. Get me an espresso kid, and a cigar to chew. Then we'll talk about your coach, and what it's going to take to make you a champ."

Chapter 2
ON TIME

Travelers moved in and out like pinballs firing at half speed. Obese people drove quiet electric scooters and filled their baskets with jerky sticks, bags of chips, and all manner of plastic wrapped sweets. Truckers with cowboy hats walked straight to what they needed, be it motor oil or chili dogs, and headed back out to their warm, idling, big rigs. Some walked around, bow legged and serious, leaving nothing more than their payments and stern nods behind. Packs of families clung to each other in their pajamas, as if they had been teleported out of their cozy beds, and into this cold, junk food driven rest stop.

The fighter maneuvered himself behind a rack of high protein cookies after noticing that the TAPTHIS! punks who hassled him in the restroom hadn't left yet.

The little brother and sister duo from the bus walked by holding hands. They were on a mission to find an original arcade game.

Aeson heard a small mechanical buzz, like gears whining before they blow apart and wondered for a second if the annoying sound was just in his own head.

———

"Yes, he'll be here by three o'clock. Uncle Sal's picking him up from the Port Authority," said Han, still masked, with his chin resting on the crown of his grandfather's head.

"And you say you picked him out of a hundred coaches, to teach you mixed martial arts?" Vincent questioned softly.

"More like two hundred Grandpa, and yes, Aeson Cadmus, is the best! He'll be world champ someday, I figured it out based on his techniques and skill, his athleticism, and of course his overall mentality. Al and Sal agree with me."

"Got to have the right mind to fight, that's for sure," replied Grandpa Vincent while reaching his arms upward and covering his grandson's hands with his own.

"I got a guy too Han. Maybe if he doesn't make the cut, you'd still like to meet him?" Vincent said softly to his grandson while staring up into his eyes.

"Really!"

"Shhh..." said Vincent while smiling up, happy that Han seemed pleased with his surprise.

Han whispers back, "Even if he doesn't sign the confidentiality agreement?"

"This guy's from the old school, he don't need to sign nothing."

The oldest and the youngest Zucharinos joined the rest of the family who were gathering around a thick wooden table. Everyone pulled out chairs in preparation for Uncle Al's breakfast banquet. A small elevator behind the bar, a dumbwaiter buzzed to signal Al's delivery.

The kiwi pancakes' scent pulled Han's chin back and his eyes closed. Al always made them just the way Han liked, everything fresh and without any animal products.

Different fruits filled the table quickly. The steaming stack was joined by tofu quiche, fruit filled muffins, cinnamon quinoa, and a citrus granola parfait that Al just happened to whip up in the wee hours of morning.

"Today's the day kid, we got two private coaches who made the cut," said Uncle Salvatore, eyeing the griddle-hot choices with trepidation.

"Yeah but Aeson Cadmus..." Han immediately rose to his pick's defense before getting cut off in mid sentence.

"Hey, you know what your mother says," Uncle Salvatore replied with an air of seriousness.

Han finished the rest of Sal's thought so quickly it was as if he was a competitor on a game show; "Life is not a matter of chance it's a matter of choice. Right?"

"That's right kid, you're a good listener, but maybe lay off the coffee," Sal said smilingly, "that was a little too quick," slightly entertained because he got his nephew riled up and awake. "And take off the mask, time to eat."

"Don't bust his chops Sal," Han's mother Stella commanded. She seemed to have materialized from the shadow of the staircase. "I know you want Aeson Cadmus for your coach honey. We've been through all this. All I'm saying is let's meet his competition before jumping to final decisions.

————

A gloved hand plucked a We're All Devils in NJ! scarf from a rack, balled it up, and pressed it into Aeson's chest. "You drop this," the anonymous female voice said to Aeson. His eyes moved back and forth wondering why a random woman had asked him to take something from her and then drop it on the ground. "On the camera. Drop this on the camera that's walking around," she directed. He responded with a searching look and wide eyes. "The one buzzing like a crowd control robot!"

"What?" Aeson replied reluctantly, still confused as to why she wanted him to cover a roving security camera. Don't have those back home, he thought to himself.

He saw the small four legged voyeur as it patrolled. The kit robot mulled around for a few seconds and started to look upwards, careening its neck to reposition its small box shaped head.

"Are you going to do it?" the strange woman asked him.

Aeson turned slowly, and reactively took the scarf as the woman's hand slid down his chest. She wore tight black gloves, a black leather jacket, and her own snow white ascot that covered much of her face in a loose mountain of soft fabric. Red hair, unnaturally fiery, sat atop her head like frozen flames. She had sunglasses on and Aeson could see his own reflection in the black lenses. Before he had time to question her strange request the woman began to make her way past Aeson while pointing downward towards the mobile security device. The whining robot's head followed her and soon its legs were moving.

Aeson's eyes tracked her and he realized that she was heading for the three trouble makers from the bathroom. He scanned the whole place as he walked towards the toy-like employee.

Aeson felt as if he was waking up from a foggy dream, like when he was on the bus. But he wasn't on the bus, he was at a rest stop, and he had a scarf in his hand.

The pills were messing with his thinking process. The scarf took a long time to fall even though it was such a short distance. It covered the robot's camera eyes completely, as well as most of its whiny metal body.

———

"Pass the syrup please."

"You got it kid. Glad you like the flapjacks flapjack."

"Whatever Uncle Al," Han said back, pouring a generous quantity of amber goodness on top of his kiwi cakes. He had switched his balaclava mask for an oversized yellow brimmed cap. Stella Zucharino placed her mug down and took hold of her son's right hand. Han's grandmother took his left. The table united in a chain and heads bowed. The large bill shadowed Han's face completely as he whispered, "Thank you Lord for this food and for our family."

"Amen!" announced Sal as he broke the link to reach for the quiche.

For at least sixty seconds the hungry family went to work on breakfast without talking. Han began to gently bounce in his chair with excitement.

"So this guy you want to be your coach is coming all the way from Colorado?" Han's grandmother asked.

"Yeah, he took the bus," Han said, smiling under his visor.

"That sounds miserable," Sal interjected between bites.

"Why does he want to teach? If he's so good, why not fight?" asked Grandma Milly, sipping tea, and looking at Sal as if to tell him to slow down.

Al poured more coffee for himself and stated, "Han's guy got in a little trouble with the commission, that's why he's available now."

Han's bouncing escalated and took on a form that did not look like happy excitement anymore.

Sal unthinkingly added to the explanation without any tact, "The kid's pick knocked out his opponent, two corner men, and the ref!"

Grandpa Vincent stepped in to give context, "We know that the other guy got kicked out too, he put chemicals on his gloves, tried to blind Han's guy."

Han's bouncing only got worse and his fork dropped onto his plate. Sal seemed to miss the queue to stop talking and Al's strong coffee made it too easy to blabber. "Guy went berserk! Wham! Bham! Like a maniac!"

"You sure about this man, Stella?" Grandma innocently asked.

"No, I'm not sure, that's why I invited my pick as well. This lady Katie Carouche, she's got it all, and no anger issues either."

Han's feet sprang to his chair. No one noticed Han's reaction from beneath the thick table at first except for his Grandma who lightly applied her palm to his back.

"Never heard of her, Stella," said Al, while dunking a muffin into a cup. "Where'd she coach?"

"All over, and she's got two master's degrees. One's in education, and one in kicking ass. Oohh, sorry Ma."

A piercing whistling sound exited from Han's throat and his feet popped up and down on top of his chair. The family realized quickly a tantrum was going to erupt if someone didn't do something quickly.

———

The three TAPTHIS! bullies had surrounded a teenage girl in the rest stop. She was obviously freaked out and looked around for someone to help. The young lady they were accosting wore a wool coat and carried a bible.

"Please save me, I've done so many bad things," the biggest one of the trio said as he put his heavy hand on her shoulder. She cringed, only to back up into a grinning pockmarked crony.

Aeson took two steps forward after he released the scarf. The red haired woman looked back and gave him a thumbs up before quickly turning and marching straight for the conflict.

"Whoa! Check this out! It's Jean Grey come to save the day!" the ringleader shouted, proud of his rhyming X-Men reference.

The woman with black gloves on and wearing a white ascot stepped smoothly in front of the terrified missionary who was traveling east for the first time. "This is the part where your little buddies start to laugh, right? About how witty you are, how clever, and strong? You're such a rare combination of leadership qualities it's almost hard to believe what will happen next."

The main offender hovered over everyone around him. Standing at six foot four inches he looked down upon the woman's robust and curly red mane. His eyes fixed on her hair and it seemed as if he had become mesmerized by the woman. He was deaf to her recriminations as well as to his team's support. His hand began to rise up and in his own mind he was super cool. He imagined his sausage-like fingers gently parting the woman's hair as he moved in for a passionate kiss.

"Not the hair!" she shouted as her right leg dropped back and set her into a deep stance. The lummox's hand hovered in space. His own face blushed, and all he heard were his sidekicks giggling.

His jaw tightened. The large and often angry man reached to put his hand upon the black leather jacket in front of him. The woman reversed her stance and stepped deeply forward with her right leg. She never changed her low defensive center of gravity. Her right fist followed her step and fired with the force of a battering ram, straight into the soft low belly of the rest stop bully. He lurched forward with a nauseating release of air. The woman spun out of the way with the grace of a reacting matador and sent the heaving giant towards the three that were standing behind her. The leader of the TAPTHIS! pack's huge boulder-like head might've crashed into the young lady with the bible if the red haired woman wearing leather had not continued to react so impressively.

Aeson did a double-take on the covered camera and saw that it was still struggling to get itself out from under the scarf. He took flight towards the situation. Before Aeson could even enter the mix the woman grabbed the falling man's pants at the beltline and put on the brakes. She placed one foot behind the large aggressive bully's knee and he came crashing down on his bottom. The man landed hard and sent out another teeth chattering gasp.

Resting her knee on the back of the downed giant's neck she turned her sights towards the other two. "Don't have anything better to do than objectify women and make fun of people who are thankfully different than you?"

Aeson at last arrived on the scene.

"Who's this, your boyfriend?"

"Some chicks like dating homeless dudes!"

"Looks like he's having a panic attack."

"You having a panic attack homeless boyfriend dude!"

Aeson hated the pills he took more than ever in that moment. He began to feel queasy and trapped in the strange chemical grip.

"I think you guys need to know that women don't need boyfriends to fight their battles anymore."

The sixteen year old missionary from Utah stepped forward and agreed with her heroine by pushing her bible into each of the two standing bullys' scrawny chests as she yelled, "Yahyah! Yahyay!"

———

"Time out honey, take a time out, I didn't mean to ..." Stella tried to apologize and looked to her brothers for help.

Han became quiet and slowly rose, feet firmly planted on the strong wooden chair's seat. The family's eyes followed upwards. He came to full stature and slowly raised both his arms in the air.

"Han… kid… relax…" Al began to stand up, ready seemingly to catch his nephew if he were to fall.

Han's head turned to Al and the glare he shot from beneath his hat's brim caused his uncle to sit back down.

Sal whispered, "Just let him be, let the kid be…"

Han's arms reached for the ceiling and his hands formed into fists. Grandma winced as if an explosion was about to occur.

Grandpa Vincent was the only one unshaken. He sipped from his green drink and made a loud slurping sound. Han almost cracked a smile then turned his eyes towards his raised hands for some sort of guidance.

"Not too long from now you'll be a teenager and this stuff will have to end," Vincent announced, not looking at anyone in particular. "Good smoothie Al, nice texture."

Han's head slowly lowered and suddenly, faster than anyone else could even blink, the youngest Zucharino beat twice with his fists on his own chest, leapt over his grandmother, away from the table, and rolled towards the glass doors of his lab. The sensors were the only things faster than Han, and they whipped the entrance open just as the rolling twelve year old was about to collide. The doors closed as quickly behind him as they opened.

Grandpa, Grandma, Stella, Al, and Sal all turned, only to see the digital glass cloud over, and then go pitch black, denying all the view to the interior of Han's private work space.

Grandma put her head in her hand as Grandpa reached across the table to comfort her. "Not your fault, he's sensitive right now. He's becoming a teenager."

"There's the scarf I was going to get you!"

"What?" asked Aeson, trying hard to go with the red haired woman's flow.

"The scarf! You must've accidentally dropped it on the little robot thing. Pick it up, let me pay for it, and we'll get going."

The sun was getting stronger and Winter was showing its first signs of surrendering. He followed the woman as directed to her car. It was a bright yellow ride, very sporty, and extremely inviting to a bus weary traveler.

"What are you waiting for? Get in man, I'll give you a lift."

"You don't even know where I'm going, and why are you being so nice?"

"Look, this is my route, and I always pass these travel busses. You're going to New York terminal, switching off, and heading to Bergen County right?"

Aeson watched the bus he rode in for over twenty-four hours rumble back to life.

"Alpine. The place I'm going is Alpine New Jersey," he said with some hesitation but sure that that's what it said on Lenora's reminder sheet.

"Yeah, Alpine's in Bergen County. Get in and we'll swing by the bus first to grab your stuff."

To pull away from the rest stop and to get back onto the last long stretch of highway felt surreal from the view of the luxury bucket seat.

"What's going on in Alpine? You doing a documentary on the rich and richer?"

"Job interview."

"Really? Housekeeping?"

Aeson took the new hockey scarf he was wearing off and rolled it into a ball, not sure what to do with it. "No, actually it's coach…" Aeson started but stopped himself when he remembered the agreement. Nobody gets to know details, especially the client's name. "You know, I better call them, let them know not to pick me up at the bus stop."

"Perfect. Go for it. You want to make a good impression before you get to your interview."

———

Han's mind ran wild with many thoughts and emotions. Butt out! Everybody! This is my life. I'm the one who can't go out in public! He paced up and down the black matted walkway. Blue lights flickered from various terminals and devices. But Grandpa's right, time to stop being a baby. I'll be thirteen in a few months and that's manhood for a lot of cultures. His pacing began to slow down and he stared through the blackened glass at his family. Vincent continued to sip his smoothy while everyone else appeared prematurely finished and on cleanup duty. I ruined everything again. And what if Aeson doesn't like me?

Han made his way down the walkway but this time didn't turn around. As he stepped into what might seem to be a dark wall, a white light lit up an entrance. Three neon letters provided by his uncles burned brightly above a door. VIP.

———

Music had begun to resonate from all around him just as Aeson hung up with Salvatore Zucharino. It wasn't loud but felt to him as if it were moving through every pore of his body.

"He said thanks and to call him if we get lost or hit traffic," Aeson let his new driver know.

"Told you, more points for you now. Well take my number too just in case."

"Sure, give me your name and I'll just…"

"Just bump phones Aeson, and all my information will be uploaded to yours."

They "bumped" phones, and a few minutes of awkward silence ensued. She turned up the music two or three notches. It sounded new age and weird but was really very relaxing. The fighter started to recall what real sleep felt like and fought the urge to curl up in a ball and start snoring.

The malls seemed never ending, and the cars were low to the ground, brightly colored, and very fast. Those things would never make it on the road to dad's cabin, he thought to himself. He knew it was barely noon, and was expecting the sun to get only brighter. The day however for Aeson Cadmus started to slowly darken.

"It's the glass Aeson, I'm shadowing the passenger side so you can relax. I want to thank you for helping me out back there. And know that me getting you to Alpine is the least I can do."

"I don't think I did much, honestly."

The lady placed her hand firmly above Aeson's knee and let it linger and grow warm before saying, "You're tough on yourself aren't you?"

"Ahhh… sometimes, I guess."

"Those pills you take making you tired?"

"How'd you know?"

"Used to work in a shrink's office. You got that sedated look. Your dosage may be too high. It's atypical actually. Does it ever swing the other way, you know akathisia or hypomania?"

"What? No. I don't think so."

"What is it? If you don't mind me asking? And how long you been on it?"

The woman with flaming red hair who still wore her sunglasses and flowing white scarf touched a button on her steering wheel and the passenger side of the car darkened fully. The seat became warmer and even reclined without Aeson doing a thing.

"Synthoanzapine. And, just shy of three weeks."

"Oh boy. You gonna let your new boss know?"

"I guess so, haven't thought about it."

"You know you've traveled a long way and don't need to think right now. You want to be well rested for your interview."

"Really? You don't mind if I close my eyes for ten minutes?"

"Make it fifteen, I'll wake you when I see paradise."

Aeson was so tired it seemed as if the woman's last word was heard by both his waking and by his sleeping self. Dice, the kind you roll on a green felt table, appeared to him in a dreamlike image. They tumbled across a sea of soft felt.

He was in Vegas and there was a celebration happening. The word "Champ!" was echoing off the poker tables and coming out of cigar clenching lips. He could see Lenora in a low cut ballroom gown. Her hair was up and her neckline appeared absolutely stunning. His girlfriend's eyes twinkled from across the room, and a faceless crowd was turned towards her elegant beauty.

"I did it. I'm the champ, now I can ask her…"

The fighter began to stand. He spent a sizable chunk of his prize money on a ring and the moment he had been dreaming of ever since he first stepped into the cage had arrived. Aeson looked down and his body was wrapped tightly in a straitjacket. The more he struggled the tighter it got. He fell to the floor and a hunk of grey cigar ashes landed on his face. Lenora's legs were visible from beneath the table and he began to crawl towards her. The more effort he put forth to move, the farther and farther away she got.

"Get up! Quick! Get up, you got to go! I got to go!"

His eyes opened and he was in the strange woman's car. The new age music turned off and the windows began to clear.

"Are we here? Is this Alpine?"

"Not exactly but you got to go! I've got to go!"

Aeson reacted as directed again and opened the door.

"Don't forget your bag Aeson!"

The woman grabbed his backpack from the back seat and threw it towards him. Still groggy, he watched as his knapsack hit pavement. It was cold, dirty, city pavement.

As he picked it up he watched the woman stretch to pull the door closed.

"Thank you… I never got your name."

"Good luck Aeson!" the woman shouted, chucking his new scarf out the window and on to the ground, apparently very pressed for time. As he stood to shoulder his pack he thought he heard her finish her goodbye with something that sounded like, "You're gonna need it."

———

Han checked his phone and realized that his mom's interview pick would be arriving shortly, but he still had time to enter the VIP. He was resistant of his mom's candidate, but naturally curious, and wanted to be ready to watch her conversation through his window to the world. Virtual reality exploring and gaming often helped calm him down when he was stressed.

V.I.P. stood for virtual, independent, and physical. These are the words that marked the most cutting edge and most real gamer's hangout of all time. It was new, burgeoning, and a myth to most. VIP was the latest thing though, and as of yet still totally non-commercial. The big companies couldn't get their hands on it because of its inability to meet any semblance of safety regulations, (that's also why Han kept it a secret from his mom). The world Han hung out in was virtual reality yes, but totally independent of the commonly accessible internet. VIP took gaming to the next, next level. Besides its virtual realism, and truly independent open source structure, it was also physical, thanks to a full body suit that only those in the underground gaming community knew how to program and manufacture.

Han pulled the suit onto his feet first. Once the booties were secured it was almost as though the form fitting outfit came alive, and climbed up the rest of his body with very little effort on his part.

The final touch, after even his face was covered, were the goggles. The eyepieces resembled a swimmer's eyewear instead of the large, older, oculus style diving mask medium.

As the door closed behind him the room became pitch. For Han however, the room brightened, not only with light and sound, but with a score of diverse and interesting people.

———

Aeson wasn't the only one watching the fancy yellow sports car zoom out of sight.

"Damn! Son just got booted! I remember when my last old lady threw me out. But on the street! That's just cold," said the voice of a man who watched Aeson's drop off happen.

"Hah! You're last old lady was so old she look like she fart out cobwebs and dust. I told her to act her age and you know what she did?" said what looked to be a woman, warm within layers of raggedy clothing. "She died! I made that joke up. You are the fool!" she finished, leaning over with hands on her knees and laughing hysterically.

The car Aeson arrived in disappeared down a side street, and towards the ever flowing and fast moving highway. A couple, homeless from appearance, stood behind Aeson talking. They began to argue. One of them was getting physical.

"You want to get dropped!" a stout Asian woman with sacs as big as tea bags under her eyes shouted to a lanky black skeleton wearing a boy's sized baseball jacket. The skeleton's wrists protruded when his fists balled up like a 1920's boxer.

"What you gonna do with those things? And you are a fool! You know my kung-fu can kill you!"

"Kung Fool! That's all you are is a Kung Fool! What you know about the martial arts! Huh! I was the one who whooped everyone's asses when they tried to shake you down! Line up bitches! Class is starting!" screamed the wiry figure.

Aeson watched in a confusion that started to morph into anxiety as the two definitely addicted people began to push, shove, fall and crawl, in a frenzy of slaps and screams.

Aeson looked away from the scramble and saw broken windows, brick buildings covered in spray painted images, and garbage strewn and stuck in fences and gutters. A dog with one clouded eye and bits missing from both his ears bounced by, having more important things to do than watch the desperate antics of two lost souls and one utterly confused fighter.

"Can you guys tell me how far Alpine is from here?"

The yellow sports car picked up speed consistently until it was away from the damaged, struggling, and impoverished neighborhoods. She smiled when she caught the image in her rearview mirror of a sign that read, Leaving Newark, Come Back Soon.

"No thanks!" she said while removing her wig. The red curls fell onto the passenger seat and she shook her blonde short hair out with abandon and delight.

———

The small padded room, full of embedded circuitry and powered by its own solar panel set that Han installed himself on their roof's tower had become a massive Viking-style virtual meeting hall once the VIP door closed.

"Wukong! It's been awhile," announced Achilles, "I needed you yesterday. Gray Faces jumped me in the *Tunnel* so I sent one of them down to Hades myself." Han didn't believe him but nodded his head in approval.

"Sure, brag about bashing a few Gray Faces. Fourth dimensional *Reptoids* tried to rip off my source code and I have the bite marks to prove it." The figure, almost translucent in appearance, shimmered when he spoke, and stared into Han's eyes with a morphing star filled expression.

"What's up Yamosha? How's it going Achilles? Glad to hear you guys are hard at work cleaning up the Tunnel. I don't go in there myself. Anyone see Katya yet?" Han asked both of the welcoming avatars.

"Not today," answered Achilles, removing his helmet, and allowing golden blonde locks to unfurl over his broad, godly, shoulders.

"Me neither, Wukong," said Yamosha who began to shift into another form, "but I could easily pretend." Color began to fill his face, along with a nose, eyes, and altogether feminine features. Four arms began to dance before Han, each holding a different ancient Indian weapon.

"No thanks Yam, I actually want to see Katya and not her impersonator. She must be busy."

Giants walked by, faeries flew, robots rolled and strolled. A queen of sorts riding a unicorn strode majestically, and brandished an enormous two handed sword on her back. Chalices were filled with something that could almost be tasted, and Odin himself seemed to be happily snoring atop a throne that overlooked it all.

"Well," said Achilles, "if she's not around, no use wasting the day moping. Let's enter one of the rooms we scouted and find some action!"

"*Donnybrook?*" asked Yamosha as he turned back into his morphing starry self.

"Let's do this. I've been tracking some New Zealand scrubs who are pretty merciless in there."

Many doors awaited the VIP players; some to basic gaming systems within the internet, some to top secret government training sites who functioned only within the *Undernet*, and some to the unknown realms of artificial intelligence's virtual, independent, and physical world. *Valhalla* was a safe room Han and some of his friends were granted access to by its owner, and that's usually where they spent most of their time. *Valhalla* was a port that led to at least one free game. It was a good game in Han's opinion that had been redesigned for the VIP platform.

After entering *Donnybrook* the three heroes appeared side by side on a moonlit field. They listened for the panting efforts of someone running for their life. Wukong held in his hands the metal pole that became a deadly cudgel in his virtual grasp. Wukong's armor was plated and allowed for flexibility. Inside the padded room in his family's basement Han stretched and moved his arms and legs. On the virtual field he was the Monkey King preparing for combat.

———

"What you mean Alpine? You making fun of us? Cause we live in Brick City! Boy you a long way from home and you about to discover the Kung-Fu of Newark!" shouted the overly shrouded, even for the end of February, homeless Chinese lady.

The pills finally started to wear off and Aeson wondered how long he slept for, and just what time it really was. Bus signs abounded so he decided to leave the belligerent greeting party and walk towards some form of transportation.

"Where you think you're going boy?" said the lanky and lean man, grabbing hold of Aeson's pack and attempting to yank him backwards into his desperate, drug hungry grasp.

Aeson felt the slight tug and allowed his body to move with the force of the pull instead of resisting it. The tall bony figure yanked as hard as he could and pulled Aeson straight back into his own unsteady frame. The once athletic man fell down with a pathetic crumbling motion and instantly began to hold his elbow as if in great pain.

"You broke my arm! Trying to rob me, he broke my arm!"

Instead of continuing his flight Aeson looked down and offered his hand to the clearly withdrawing and utterly tormented soul. Surprised by Aeson's resistance to violence, the raggedy couple backed away from further harassments, but as Aeson left to find another bus stop they continued to follow him.

Aeson sat down at another bus stop bench and looked at his phone. The tweaking pair sat with him and talked to themselves more than they did to each other. They scratched at invisible insects and raked their arms more raw. Aeson felt their bodies shaking and heard one of them grinding their teeth.

The power was off on his phone, and all he could seem to access was a blank black screen. He tried and tried to ignite the digital flame within the cellular device, but to no avail.

It hit him like a baseball bat in the spine. He was going to miss the interview and had no way of letting the family know. Anger for falling asleep, for not staying on the bus, and for taking those damn pills unquestioningly made him nothing short of enraged. He grabbed the pharmaceuticals out of his pocket, and squeezed the plastic jar tightly, trying to decide what to do.

"What you got there man? One of your multi-millionaire gizmos? It gonna turn into a helicopter and get you to Alpine!"

The two shook with laughter, and to his surprise, Aeson began to laugh too.

"Naw, nothing special, just some Synthoazapine," Aeson answered.

The two looked at each other questioningly. The one of exceptional height, who sported a pick in his hair and foot movement that made it seem like he was once a real fighter, made a proposal.

———

Back in the VIP room, goggles off and game over, Han wiped the sweat from his eyes. His arm muscles already felt sore from the virtual metal pole he had recently dispatched opponents with. The suit bubbled and slid with micro movements guided by nano-bots within the clothing's fiber. It was a fun time, but Han wished Katya could have been there. He really just wanted to hang out with her in the great hall, and to let her know, without revealing too much, all the struggles he was going through, and how nervous he was over the big change that was about to come into his life.

Showered and back in his Ambercrombie wardrobe, Han sipped on a can of pineapple juice. When he got to the blackened out door the woman was already there, and in mid-conversation with his mom. Han sat cross legged and observed.

Stella seemed excited to have another woman besides her mother in the house. Han's uncles, even though Aeson was their first choice, appeared to be having the same reaction.

"So you watch a lot of MMA?" asked Sal while trying not to look anywhere else except the applicant's eyes.

"I fought MMA actually, in college. Yale had great academics as well as a lot of strong fighters."

"Wow, Yale, with all that opportunity, why did you get into fighting?" Stella asked before taking another sip of her tea.

"There's something primal about fighting that just puts me in the moment. It is martial arts though that can harness that energy, and turn it into something productive," spoke the clearly impressive applicant.

Al wrote things down on a pad of paper to look impressive, not revealing his shopping list or the veggie burger recipe he was actually working on. "What's your take on special needs kids? My nephew is very gifted, but has his quirks that tend to need a unique style and attention."

Han began to bounce in his private room, offended slightly, but too tired after his VIP session to get enraged.

"My philosophy Mr. Zucharino..."

"Call me Al, please."

"My philosophy Al, is that all kids are special, and sometimes it just takes the right coach to bring out their best attributes."

The Zucharinos nodded in agreement. Han realized that the interview was at its tail end, and that this lady before him, attractive as any he'd ever seen on the cover of his mom's magazines, must have done a stellar job.

"Where is your nephew, by the way Al?" she asked, "I can't wait to meet him."

Han moved back instinctively, and checked that the lock on his door was activated.

Stella stepped in almost involuntarily, "He's shy, Miss Carouche, very shy."

"Please, call me Katie."

"He's a nervous kid Katie, and works at his own pace when it comes to social situations."

"I see," Katie Carouche responded, realizing that she would not see Stella's son until hired, and that her interview and access to their house was about to end. She let her eager curiosity consume her and began to look around.

Han picked up on her investigation and stood to get a closer look.

Katie Carouche's eyes settled on his room's shadowed door, and she seemed to intently stare, as if she were to concentrate hard enough she might be able to see through the darkness.

Sal searched his mind for another potent question, one that might impress the beautiful applicant. Uncle Al furiously designed a cake pattern for Han's next birthday, while Stella, her maternal antennas beginning to buzz, looked back towards Han's hidden realm. They both noticed Carouche's hand touch the side of her stylish eyeglasses, but it was Han who saw through the lens of the digital glass door that their guest had activated an infrared vision sensor on one of her own lenses. Stella stood to block her way as covertly as possible while looking back towards Han as if to say, "Hide! Something is wrong!"

Han didn't need his mom's cue. He popped out of his cross legged seat and rolled backwards, not stopping until he was back in the warm, dark VIP room.

Chapter 3
FACE TO FACE INTERVIEW

"We can trade you two a those pills you got for a phone call," the skin pulled over bones told Aeson.

"Pills? My anger medication?"

"Oh no, that's not just anger management stuff…" the man continued, as if he had prepared a sales pitch for just that moment, only to be cut off by his heavily bundled companion.

"That's the stuff that can help us both get straight, it's what we need to withdraw the right way, to get clean off street drugs."

Aeson read the label on the bottle of the medication he was prescribed. It didn't say anything about helping drug addicts get clean but at this point he was feeling open to new possibilities.

"How do I know you're not just going to swallow them and then leave me stranded?"

"Because we are warriors, students of martial arts, we research our own experience man," the man's wrists moved out of the small jacket's sleeves, like fast growing twigs, and reached for what Aeson held in his hands. The fighter snatched them quickly and slid down towards the other end of the bench.

"Research your own experience? I've heard that somewhere," Aeson pondered out loud.

"Bruce Lee, stupid!" the small woman responded from beneath down, and wool, and cotton rags.

"Easy honey, this man is like us, aren't you? You a martial artist?"

Aeson stood to retrieve Lenora's sheet and to reexamine his situation. "I am a martial artist. I've been into it ever since my father showed me *Enter the Dragon*."

"Of course! I could tell by your hands, and your ugly face. A martial artist researches his own experience," said the tall man. "So you've got to ask yourself, how do you feel about helping us out? Because we both want to get back on the path. Don't we baby?"

The woman responded by discarding several articles of clothing that were stacked atop her shoulders. She stood at attention and closed her eyes. Her knees bent. She raised her arms and slapped her palms together. She jumped to her knees and the man winced, then smiled and nodded to make up for his concern. She rolled, kicked, swung, and rolled some more. When it looked as if she was going to hurt herself Aeson intervened, "Alright! Stop! I see you're... trying." Aeson clicked the bottle open and took two pills out. "Here, take one each."

The woman was sweating profusely now and panting. She scurried over and cut in front of her boyfriend.

Both pills fell to the pavement and the couple followed them down.

———

The Alpine, New Jersey mansion was in a panic. Everybody but Han had moved into the upstairs kitchen.

"Was she paparazzi?" Stella questioned dramatically while staring into the driveway from behind a thick curtain.

"Oh my God Stella. Did she have a hidden camera?" Grandma whispered while clutching Rosary beads in both her hands.

"Told you I should've frisked her Al," said Sal shaking his head and looking at his worried mother with open arms.

"Easy guy! She didn't have a camera!" shouted Al in return, "And the days of frisking guests have been over for a long time."

"Apparently not, Al!" shouted Sal back.

"We could still get my guy here ya know," said Grandpa, still calm, and sitting with his hands folded on the kitchen table.

"No offense, Pop," started Sal, "but your guy is probably older than you."

Before Grandpa could react, Al instinctively backed his brother's opinion, "Yeah Pop, let's be realistic here."

"I can still kick both your asses!" yelled their father, sending the two a few steps back.

"Vincent! Your pressure," Grandma reminded.

Sal began to lose his macho demeanor now that his mother had become visibly upset. Whenever Sal lost his cool he began to talk to himself; "I knew it, I told you, stick with the plan, just like Pop taught us, stick to the plan and everything works out…"

"Plan!" Stella winced as she heard the word come out of her own mouth. "You bums! What are you up to!"

"What plan!" Al shouted back, feigning ignorance, "He meant we should have stuck with the kid's pick, that's all!"

"They're up to something, Stella," Grandma whispered to her only daughter.

"Ma, c'mon," pleaded Al, "The kid checked his pick's background better than the FBI could, that's all he meant, c'mon Ma, don't be upset. There was no camera. I'm making cannoli today. Dairy free, for the kid."

"Whatevah…" Stella finished, with a cold disapproving glare. "I know they're up to something Ma."

While they argued upstairs Han turned the lights down in his private space and lay back on the floor. He was suddenly tired, and felt like he might cry. He wanted to get up, go to the refrigerator, and get his injection, but fatigue was overtaking him. He closed his eyes and tried to rest. Who was that weird lady he wondered, and how long until Aeson gets here?

———

Katie Carouche exceeded the speed limit. She hurled her car into a turn at close to 100 mph. She closed her eyes, let go of the wheel, and allowed the car's computer to take over. The bright vehicle spun and the safety sensors took over, righted the sports car, and avoided even a scratch. It came to a standstill and Carouche sat in darkness. The center console lit up with text and she opened her eyes.

What happened? Did you get the job? Did you see him?

Carouche looked into the green screen and tapped out her reply on the keyboard above the emergency brake.

It didn't go as planned. He didn't show himself. I'm sorry.

The console's glow became irritating to look at and Carouche began to chew on the knuckles of her right hand. When she felt her boss was finished and that there would be no more communication she took hold of the screen and turned it around. The back of the console was well padded and had the marks of use. She started the ignition, got on the road, and punched the makiwara training board with her right fist as she drove with her left. Her foot lay heavy on the pedal and her punches got harder and harder.

———

"No phone huh?" the tall skinny man asked.

"It's dead, I think the lady who..." Aeson began to explain.

"We don't use phones either, radiation, messes with the chi," he stated, licking his gums for the remnants of the pill that he pulverized with his teeth. "But I know where we could get one."

"I really need to make a call. Can you at least tell me if there are any public phones around?" the fighter, beginning to despair, pleaded.

"Hmmmm..." the lady said, still breathing heavily, "you could buy a disposable, but ain't no store's around here. Stores don't last long round here. We know somebody with a phone though."

Someone shouted at them from across the street; "Hey! Junkies! You gonna introduce us to your little white friend?"

Aeson pocketed the pills and put one hand on his backpack. What's next, he wondered. And how am I ever going to get to Alpine?

———

Han dreamed the sweet animal dreams that his injections often stifled. He floated within a green canopy, and soft primal sounds came out of his mouth. A food patch presented itself. Multi colored fruit hung before him and he heard himself squeal in delight.

"Hey kid! You want me to get you something to eat? Your guys gonna be here soon ya know," Uncle Al let Han know without barging in on him.

"Yeee! Yeee! Wyeeeyah!" Han sounded off as he rose from sleep, surprising himself when he heard his dream's voice in the waking world.

"Han! You OK?" Al asked as he slid the glass door open.

Han rubbed his eyes and yawned, then looked at Uncle Al. Han tilted his head slowly without breaking his gaze. It was as if he didn't recognize his uncle anymore.

"Kid? What are you up to?"

Han's eyes grew more intense as they drank in the world, and his lips curled upward as much as they could curl to become an excited and mischievous smile. "Yeeee! Yeeee!" he screeched out, showing the entirety of his teeth and throat.

"Sal! Get down here!" Al commanded while turning towards the main room. Al knew that he needed to get to the small refrigerator behind the bar before his nephew could.

Han was too fast, and too long without his weekly gene therapy injection. Before Al knew it he was standing in a very dark room. Han locked the door with his palm's signature, leaving Al to stumble around for the exit.

The now wide awake twelve year old howled again, tremendously pleased with his first act of rascality. "Yeee! Yeee!"

In a single leap Han was on top of the pool table, from there he bounced to the bar and removed the already full syringe. Before Al could get his cell phone out to warn the others Han was already rolling out onto the kitchen's floor. He screamed laughingly with all his might.

———

"What's next?" Aeson asked himself cautiously.

"What's next is give us the rest of those tasty treats and we'll have no trouble," said the squat, drug starved lady.

"Couple more treats like Lulu said and we'll cover your ass," spoke the man, who seemed less jittery but still full of the hunger.

"Tasty treats! What you dealing in our hood cracker!" shouted a raspy voice from behind a high leather collar. He had five cohorts with him, and by the time Aeson stood up they were already surrounding him.

"I'm not dealing anything. I'm just waiting for a bus," Aeson let them know with his returned calm demeanor.

"Well, you'll be waiting a long time, cuz the next bus that stops here is tomorrow morning. Now! String Bean and Rice Ball, what did he give you!"

"Synthoazapine," the homeless couple answered in chorus.

"Really? My word. Big pharma has arrived," the threatening man commented facetiously.

Aeson heard knuckles popping and limbs warming up beneath leather and denim. They were about to start swinging. Aeson wondered to himself if more than one of them would break their hand on his head. He knew at least the first guy to throw a punch would suffer.

Something must have come over the tall lanky drug addicted man. A memory of a nobler time came upon him perhaps, and for a moment, he became his former self; "We were just researching our own experiences, Walter, that's all, this guy's not dealing, we just…"

"Shut up!" And with that a fist swung violently towards the rail thin nomad. Aeson retaliated, like a soccer goalie blocking a power shot, and intercepted the attacker's fist with the crown of his own head.

Crunch! would have been a sickening sound, if Aeson were still operating on his prescribed medications. Now the noise only made him coolly smile, and do what he always did best, fight.

The sucker puncher held his injury as he dropped to one knee in utter pain. Aeson pressed one foot on top of the attacker's hunched back. He pushed off as if he were using the tree stump his father trained him to do flying techniques from. Aeson was in the air and delivering a knockout blow to the group's second in command. The fighter landed squarely on his feet as the second man dropped. The homeless couple pulled themselves away, but with two thugs down they stayed for the show. A third, now with more time to prepare, began to retrieve something from his jacket. Aeson's side kick knocked him backwards and onto his butt before his hand could access the weapon. Aeson followed up with a spinning round house from his other leg, which landed on the fourth man's jaw, knocking him unconscious before he hit the sidewalk. The fifth assailant, without any support and in a state of shock from the rapidity of this stranger's defenses, screamed in a panicked kamikaze fashion, only to be summarily silenced with a classic left right punching combo. The man who had went for his knife had his hands in the air, while the leader, still clutching his fractured limb, shouted insults.

"I just need to make a phone call. Can somebody get me to a phone?" Aeson asked, directing his voice towards the spectating couple.

Lulu and her boyfriend Jacob began to experience emotions that they had thought long since burned away.

"Come with us," Lulu said as she took tall Jacob's hand.

"You really do your research! A real martial artist. So we are going to take you to the right place," Jacob said.

———

"Give me that injection right now Han Zucharino!" Stella yelled, doing her best to balance authority with natural logic. Han just laughed crazily and with so much gusto that it took his own mother by surprise.

"Sal, how did this happen!"

"I'm on it!" Sal shouted as he popped out from behind the door in hopes of getting the jump on his wild nephew.

Han, instead of being scared and caught off guard, took it as a playful move and became even more excited. He easily evaded his uncle's grasp by ducking and disappearing under the table, landing right at his grandmother's feet. Han popped his head up between her knees and into her lap. She screamed with surprise and Han let out his loudest "Yeeeeee!" smiling broadly now and showing all of his teeth.

"Vincent! Han needs his shot!" Grandma cried.

"Whaa! Whaa!" was Grandpa Vincent's reaction to his wife's signal. Vincent's high hoot sound made his grandson freeze before he disappeared again.

Han ran on two feet and one hand, the other hand held his weekly treatment aloft.

"Whaa! Come here Han. Whaa... that's it, whaa..." with each stride closer Vincent became quieter with his own primal sounds and with his words. Han responded by slowing to a trot. He moved slowly into the room where the familiar kind voice of his grandfather came from. Vincent sat in a chair and looked out into the backyard through a large window. His voice became a whisper as Han's feet pressed against the soft carpeting. "Whaa.... whaa... whaa, come on in kid. Come to Grandpa, and I'll help you with that."

Han began to grow tired again and his head began to hang as he approached Vincent.

"It's OK," his grandfather sincerely let him know. "Let Grandpa help you."

Han reached for his grandfather, and Vincent embraced him. Taking him under the armpits Vincent hoisted his grandson on top of his lap.

Han surrendered the syringe tiredly and wrapped both arms affectionately around his grandpa's neck.

"Don't worry kid, Grandpa's gonna take care of you," he said as he cleared the shot for any air bubbles before carefully poking, then injecting his grandson in the arm with the solution. Han winced for a moment, closed his eyes, and then as if transformed, spoke in a calm voice, "What happened Grandpa? Did I break anything?"

"Everything's fine Han. Everything's going to be fine now," Vincent replied, looking towards the door and at the relieved expressions of the four other members of the Zucharino household.

———

Aeson followed the pair down the street, through an alley, over a fence, and finally up to the front door of the location they intended to bring him to. The metal portal was painted with a black and white Ying/Yang symbol and read Dao Jang of Jeet-Kune-Do.

Aeson wasn't sure if the two were even rational, but was glad that the altercation had seemed to drive the chemicals fully out of his own system. Besides feeling lost in a foreign place, tricked by a strange woman, and guilty for being late to his interview, Aeson began to regret ever having taken the doctor's orders. Why didn't I get a second opinion, he pined to himself. Why didn't I refute the commission? I never needed that stinking medicine.

Jacob knocked, and as they waited for a reply. Aeson could smell incense wafting from the mail slot. He heard the peep hole's cover turn, and stood up straight, knowing that someone was watching.

The heavy door opened. "Jacob, Lulu, and whoever you are, take a step back, so I can see who's knocking so loudly at the door of our school," said a man, who was equally as tall as Jacob, and resembled Jacob in every way besides disrepair and addiction.

Lulu and her man tilted their heads downward to bow and Lulu spoke, "Hi Sifu. This guy, he's good, not like us. He's lost, and needs to make a phone call."

"Can't he speak for himself? You really want these two pillars of society speaking for you Mister?" the Sifu asked Aeson sternly.

"I am sorry to bother you. Things have gotten a little strange for me lately, and I'm supposed to be in Alpine, NJ within the hour for a job interview. I've travelled a long way. My name is..."

"I think I know your name son. Cadmus right? Aeson Cadmus, kicked out of your last fight league, I believe," responded the Sifu.

"If you saw the fight you would know that..."

"Oh I saw it. I know you got the short end of the stick, even though you do need to keep that anger in check. Been the downfall of many a good fighter. My only question is, why didn't you fight the suspension? Clearly the other guy was in the wrong. I would've done the same thing if somebody tried to burn my eyes just cause I was winning a fair fight," the Jeet Kune Do teacher let Aeson know, sending a wave of warm feelings through the fighter's body. "Now what the hell you doing in this neighborhood with Miss Lulu and my big brother?"

———

"You forgot to take your therapy kid, that's all. We'll remind you next time."

"Sorry Grandpa, I thought everything was under control, but I didn't sleep a lot last night, and that woman..."

"We're gonna find out who she was, don't you worry."

"She couldn't have been one the fundamentalists? Right Grandpa?" Han fearfully asked.

"Like Grandpa said, kid," Sal spoke from the doorway, "We're going to find out who she is, and take care of it."

Han apologized to everyone, and par the course, no one made him feel badly. Everyone around him understood Han's condition, but it didn't remove Han's shame, or his worry that it would happen again. Things were tidied, and the house made ready for the interview everyone was looking forward to. By this time Aeson was fifteen minutes late and not answering his phone. Everyone tried to erase the weirdness of the day so far and attempted to summon the excitement that was buzzing in the household before Katie Carouche's bothersome exit.

"He'll be here Han," Al told him. "Those roads are a nightmare. Your guy's ride probably got stuck in traffic."

Han let himself be reassured until Aeson's lateness began to exceed the one hour mark.

Grandma brought out cookies and poured tea, but nobody felt like eating. None of them realized how quiet the Zucharino house had become either, until the buzzer on the driveway gate sounded. Al buzzed the car through.

The "bling" chime Sal installed seemed to shake the whole house, and suddenly everyone realized that Han's pick might very well have made it. Stella smoothed out her dress and checked her makeup in the hallway mirror. Grandma rearranged the tea cups one more time and the uncles both looked at Han as if to ask him what he wanted to do. Han removed himself from sight but kept within earshot.

Vincent signaled Stella to get the door.

The chime rang again and Han's mom shook off the last remains of a strange day.

Han peered from beneath a curtain into the driveway and was surprised to the point of being shocked when he gazed upon a car that looked like a 1966 model Imperial Crown sedan, identical, minus the hood mounted machine guns, to Green Hornet's Black Beauty. The driver even looked like he could have been a martial arts superstar from the 60's, sporting hefty sideburns, and stiff curly hair that could store its own pick. As the car disappeared out of the driveway and through the open metal gates Han slunk quietly back towards the shadows.

Throughout the process Han followed along invisibly. When they went downstairs he took the back way down and headed into his personal lair so that he could look again, and from behind the darkened glass door.

Aeson looked just like he did on TV and seemed to act just like his uncles said he would. They had convinced him months before of Aeson's qualifications, and all thought it a fortuitous misfortune when the fighter lost his day job.

Everyone bombarded him with the same questions that they had asked the woman. None of Aeson's answers seemed rehearsed, and his lack of words was made up for by his authenticity.

After feeling satisfied with all of his responses, Mrs. Zucharino asked the inevitable interview question; "Do you have anything to ask us?" Aeson's reply put Han in the most profoundly responsible position of his life.

"Can I meet your son now?"

Silence fell over the party, and before Grandpa could again offer the fighter an espresso, the darkened glass door slid open.

All eyes turned towards Han. He straightened his back as much as he could, but kept his hat's brim pulled down. Han walked with his hands behind his back and slowly, one slipper wearing foot at a time, approached. Aeson began to eye his potential student with wonder and began to walk towards him as well.

The family hadn't expected Han to show himself so early, and fought to let their son, nephew, and grandson be allowed to act on his own.

Before they were a foot apart Aeson reached out his own hand to shake. Han, keeping his head prostrate, unclasped his fingers from behind his back. Aeson kept himself calm and knew that this was a special moment for the boy who stood before him, and possibly for himself. As Han's arm came forward Aeson's eyes grew big with utter surprise. It took everything in his power to try and comprehend the strange appendage that reached out to grasp his hand. The boy had five very hairy, or rather furry, fingers. The hair, like his fingernails, were jet black. Aeson took the boy's hand into his and it felt rougher than leather, like the raw hide his father always had laying around his cabin. The grip was powerful for a twelve year old. Aeson's eyes followed up past the boy's wrist, and even though he wore long sleeves Aeson knew the kid was exceptionally strong. Finally, without

44

letting go, Han began to lift his eyes. Aeson wanted to bend and peer beneath Han's hat brim but demonstrated self-restraint. As the kid's head lifted Aeson became filled with utter shock, and even his fighter's heart began to skip. Movies, books, stories, could not match what was before the twenty three year old MMA contender from Colorado. Aeson's entire sense of reality, momentarily, bent and twisted itself, and the fighter felt utterly awed and humbled. Before him, shaking his hand, stood a boy who was for all intents and purposes not just a boy. Specifically Han Zucharino as could be learned by his wide hand-like feet, his small shiny black eyes, and his overall jolly but simian structure, was a hybrid; human, but at the same time, ape.

Chapter 4
HIRED

"Would anyone like a cannoli?" Grandma asked quite innocently, "Alexander made his nephew's favorite treat. No sugar either, just how Han likes it."

Han's head bowed deeper to hide more of himself, and his hand slid slowly out of Aeson's.

The round table, usually loud and jovial, became filled with tender silence. Aeson realized that his stomach was loudly grumbling. He hadn't had anything in it for almost a full day. Aeson looked down at the crusty, cream filled tube on his plate. He gazed up and his eyes scanned worried faces. He almost laughed. He was in New Jersey, in a gated mansion, where he might have just gotten hired to teach a kid who was actually not just a kid, but an ape kid. And he was going to have a cannoli for the first time in his life. He wanted to tell Lenora about everything all of a sudden, but then remembered the confidentiality agreement stuff.

Aeson reached for his phone. All the eyes shifted and any chewing seemed to stop. He placed the phone on the table next to his plate and Han nearly ducked. Sal and Al inhaled in sync and Grandma spilled some of her tea. Grandpa just closed his eyes. Stella's long colorful fingernails drummed against her mug with an insect-like percussion. Aeson scanned the group and slowly removed his hand.

"I just want to let my girlfriend know that I made it here, that's all. But... my phone's fried."

Han's mother Stella seemed to awaken, as if a small splash of clean water hit her in the face.

"Of course, Mr. Cadmus, use our phone. Here," Stella plucked her phone from her pocket and prepared to dial, "give me her number, I'll do it for you."

Her elaborate fingernails did not impede her. She dialed as quickly as Aeson could speak. To Aeson's surprise Lenora answered and Stella began talking.

Han's embarrassment grew and he slid so low on his chair he almost fell on the floor.

"Hi! This is Stella Zucharino and I just want you to know your boy-friend has arrived and we are excited!"

A tinge of embarrassment began to climb up the fighter's neck like a tarantula. He was supposed to be a man who was striking out on his own. He looked down at his plate for the now smiling faces were too much to bear. The cannoli was light and solid feeling when he picked it up. When he bit into it, it exploded in a cloud of vegan cream and cheese. Han's eyes met Aeson's dessert covered face. Aeson couldn't look at anyone but the flustered kid. They both smiled.

"You've never been to the East Coast! Ma! Lenora's never seen New Yawk!" Stella shouted, barely turning her head away from the phone.

Grandma shook her head back and forth with her tea in her hand and spoke to herself, "Everybody's got to see the Big Apple, I mean c'mon, it's magic in fact…"

Sal, hearing his mother's solo conversation unconsciously began his own diatribe, "New York, nothing like it, capital of the world, the epicen-ter of…"

"My little Han's gonna learn how to fight. Helluva left hook already, with the right training this kid…" Grandpa Vincent began his own rev-erie.

Aeson cleaned the agave sweetened crumbs from his hands and face and tried the tea. When he put his cup down Al too was conversing with himself; "I'd like to do thirteen layers, but thirteen, c'mon, either got to do twelve, or fourteen, like the floors in the Empire State building…"

Aeson and Han were the only silent ones. Han waited until he knew Aeson was looking at him then mouthed the word, "Sorry."

Aeson mouthed back, "It's cool."

"Oh don't worry, Aeson can stay with us. Everything's ready, much bettah than any of the apartments around here. Seriously honey, we'd prefer it if he stays here, and so can you. Let us know sweetie, you're room will be waiting. And, I'm going to text you the Babazuke's 50% off coupon. We also have a great cosmetics line if you're good on supplements. Okay Lenora, take care love."

Stella hung up and entered the mix of self-talking right away; "Sweet kid. She's got to visit. We can take her to the city when she visits. You and her can stroll Central Park together. Very romantic in Spring. Of course the Jersey shore is beautiful, but that's summer."

"How about me?" asked Han. "When you guys go to New York, do you think I can come?"

No one responded right away. Aeson knew their answer. "Of course honey," Stella claimed, "we'll have a great time visiting the old neighborhood."

"There ain't nothing great about the old neighborhood Stella, especially now," said Sal.

"Don't put down where we grew up! You disrespect Ma and Pa!" shouted Stella, probably more mad at herself for lying to Han.

"Oh! Calm down Sis, we got a guest, remember?" said Al, looking for his notebook to start sketching in again.

"Don't talk to your sistah that way Alexander, she's got a point, don't forget your roots," defended Grandma.

Sal should have probably used his mother's words as a way to stop an argument, but instead he fed the flames; "Who's forgetting their roots? Every day I thank God I don't live in those roots anymore…"

Stella slammed her mug on the table, which splashed a warm shot of coffee onto the fighter's phone. Aeson picked up his napkin and wrapped the phone in it to dry. The fighter dried it thoroughly. When Aeson was done he realized everyone had stopped arguing and was silently staring at him again.

"Why'd you let your phone go dead Aeson?" Grandpa asked, ending the awkward staring contest.

"Mr. Zucharino..." the fighter began to respond.

"Please, call me Vincent."

"Vincent."

"Why'd you let your phone go dead?"

"My phone. Oh no, I didn't let it go dead. See, I took this ride from this lady at a rest stop. She ended up bumping my phone then dropping me off in Newark."

"Lady?" Uncle Al questioned, looking at Sal fearfully.

"Yeah, she's a fighter too. I thought she was cool. I was so tired I guess I fell asleep in her car. But before she left we bumped phones to exchange numbers. Next thing I know I'm stranded in Newark."

"He's trusting Stella, too trusting," Grandma said to her daughter in a voice that was significantly louder than a whisper.

"I can't believe he took a ride from a strange lady," Stella replied. Both acted as if no one could hear them.

The fighter looked over at Han as if to ask him, "They know I'm sitting here right?"

Han shrugged his shoulders, just wanting to hear more of Aeson's tale, and to forget about his loud, crazy, over caffeinated family for a little while. Han was starting to make a connection, and his curiosity began to grow. Grandma too began to think that maybe the woman who interviewed for the coaching job, the person who was in their house and standing no more than fifteen feet from her precious, and very special grandson, was the same woman who sabotaged Aeson. She gripped her palms around her cup, as if to warm them, and put her tea down. Grandma reached over and placed her hand on her husband's shoulder. She whispered in Vincent's ear and Grandpa's posture straightened.

"And who was that who gave you a lift here? Who got you out of Newark?" asked Vincent, more focused on his investigation than ever.

"Sifu Harris, a Kung-fu instructor, he..."

"You mean Jeet-Kune-Do, not exactly Kung-Fu," Han corrected somewhat mechanically; "fought from 2012 to 2015. Destroyed the amateur ranks, had only two pro fights, won both, then fell off the map."

"Kid's got a knack for tracking fighters," Sal said proudly.

"Picks 'em better than you can Sally," said his brother.

Han grinned widely revealing all his teeth. If he wasn't smiling, his large incisors and even larger canines might have been intimidating.

"Aeson," Grandpa said, bringing the group back again to the subject at hand, "what else can you tell us about the lady who stranded you and bumped your phone?"

"Hmmm... red hair, drives a yellow car, and..." Stella audibly gasped at that moment, interrupting Aeson's description.

Al and Sal stared at each other with rekindled paranoia.

Grandma warmed her hands again and placed one atop Stella's.

"What else do you know about this woman, Aeson?" Grandma softly asked.

Aeson flashbacked to the rest stop and the large man she dropped with one punch and said, "She hits really hard."

————

Katie Carouche's fast car slowed down to a crawl as it entered the long, winding Upstate New York driveway.

Gates closed behind her. They were significantly larger than the ones that guarded the Zucharino's house. The vehicle slid into a hangar sized garage. She turned the ignition off, then moved the hitting board back into position. The room lit up slowly, and eventually became filled with a white industrial light. She closed her eyes and exhaled, summoning strength. An electronic dog greeted her as she got out. She pushed the door closed and tried to not look the metal creature directly in its camera eyes. It was no kit robot. She knew the man she took orders from was watching her, and she rehearsed her explanation one last time in her head.

————

Han gave Aeson a tour of the house. When they got to the gym Aeson began to feel at home. Aeson had seen a lot of training equipment over the years, but some of the machines in the Zucharino's house were actually new to him. State of the art was an understatement.

"Most of the equipment is promotional. Our family company Babazuke Health Products does business with all these manufacturers, so they hook us up with their beta test gear."

Aeson noticed that many of the punching bags and practice dummies were damaged and torn to the point of being useless. He wondered just how much power this special kid could generate.

Although exhausted from travel and strange adventure, the fighter felt a strong urge to begin training. It was the core of his existence, and the only thing that made him feel truly whole. He wanted to kick, punch, lift, run, and sweat.

He looked at his new student in the wall sized mirror's reflection. Han walked upright, but Aeson could tell it was not the kid's most comfortable stride. What kind of a creature is he, the fighter wondered? Aeson had felt different his whole life. The fighter grew up poor, and with a father who gave new meaning to the word antisocial. Things were never easy. His struggles, though, couldn't compare to the kid's. The kid was going to have an uphill battle, and Aeson worried that he wouldn't have enough to offer him. The Zucharinos hired a martial arts instructor however, and for the next six months, Aeson promised, that is what they're going to get.

"Your training starts tomorrow you know."

"O.K."

"Bright and early."

"O.K."

"Are you ready to become a fighter?"

"I think so."

"Don't think."

"Don't think? How am I supposed to do that?"

"You're already over thinking it Han. Just be, you know, be yourself."

"How can I be anything but myself?"

"You know what I mean, just be. Do what truly makes you happy."

"Want to play a video game?"

"Hey kid!" It was Sal shouting. "You going to let the guy settle in or what. I know we're paying him a lot of money, but have a heart."

"Sorry Aeson. I can show you your room," said Han apologetically.

"You got it Han, lead the way," answered the fighter.

Sal blocked the exit with his body; "I didn't mean to break up the tour now guys."

"It's fine Sal, we're going to get a fresh start in the morning," said Aeson.

"Naw, it's early. Listen, the kid's got cool games. *Donnybrook*'s the best, enjoy yourselves," said Sal. "But... did you take his stats yet, to get ready for training?"

"Stats? You mean like height and weight and stuff?" Aeson clarified.

"Exactly, smart guy. But we got sensors that measure punching power, kicking speed, even body fat. In a few months we'll compare and contrast the kid's growth."

"Sounds like a good idea," said Aeson.

They walked to the scale, only instead of Han getting on, Sal asked Aeson to. "Hold still guy. Hold it..." The scale read not only his weight, but given the time, it recorded overall mass, reach, neck thickness, foot measurements, quick twitch muscle sensitivity, and even cellular water retention.

An electric cloud seemed to form around Aeson and he felt as if every hair on his body stood on end.

"What's your blood type Aeson?" asked Sal as he stepped away from the buzzing body analysis platform.

"My bloodtype?"

"Just in case," Sal informed.

"In case of what Sal?" asked Aeson.

"In case you got into an accident," Han completed.

"Maybe it's time to show your coach to his room?" said Sal to his nephew.

Aeson was eager to see and feel his new bed, but wondered why his own measurements even mattered.

———

"I need the gene treatment sir, and I need it tonight," said Katie Carouche, her words directed at the robot dog.

The lights in the echo filled space shut off instantly and with a slamming sound. A voice resonated from the four legged machine's speakers, "You do not make demands! I do! You came to me for help!"

Katie Carouche knelt on one bent knee and whispered fearfully towards the robot, "I will get what you need, I have a plan. But please, give me what I need sir."

The metal dog stood motionless and Carouche waited, still kneeling, for its answer. Its eyes aglow with blue, created an orb of light around her and the machine.

"You have another day to show me something."

She followed the robot with her eyes as it ungraciously strode away.

Katie Carouche's foot became heavy on the pedal as soon as the garage door opened. She punched it in reverse, hit a 180, and sped through the enormous iron gates before they were fully opened.

When she keyed into her apartment a man came to the door. Carouche wasn't startled, and whispered, "Did everything go alright while I was gone?"

"Of course my dear, as always we had a nice time, and everything is fine. Any luck for you?" he asked, with his R sound coming out more like L.

"Not exactly," she whispered, "well sort of," she slipped her shoes off and looked eagerly towards the back room. "It's a long story actually."

"Perhaps over tea tomorrow?"

"Yes Mr. Senga, of course," she said, and her whisper trailed off as she disappeared into the darkened back room. When she emerged she bore a look of relief, and exhaustion.

"I have set your dinner on your nightstand," the soft spoken older Japanese man let her know as he exited the small apartment complex.

Katie Carouche whispered, "Domo," as the door to her sparse and cell-like room closed. After washing her hands and face, she stared into the mirror for a moment. She opened the medicine cabinet to get skin cream for her knuckles and saw the pair of dog tags. She picked them up for a moment and rubbed her fingers over them. She grasped them tightly in her fist before placing them back in their resting place. After getting into comfortable clothes, she hopped on her grey sheeted bed, opened her laptop, and set to work.

She typed: **Hey Monkey King, you around?**

———

"This is your room Aeson," Han said as he opened the door and got out of the way. He seemed happy and eager to show the fighter what was waiting for him.

"Wow! This is where I'm staying?"

"If you don't want to get an apartment we understand. Uncle Al said rents are high and six month leases aren't easy to find."

"This is perfect Han, thanks."

Aeson never had his own room, in fact, when he lived with his mom, the whole apartment was one room. His dad's place was a cabin with an outhouse.

"Mom said if you don't like the art we can take it down."

"No way, I like being watched over by Rhonda Rousey, Bruce Lee, and ..."

"That's Sun Wukong, my avatar. Most know him as the Monkey King."

"Like Jet Li's character in the movie? Gets in trouble a lot, but ends up saving the day right?"

"Something like that."

Aeson showered and felt as if he finally cleaned off the journey. He wanted to call Lenora later but his phone was still without any sign of life. He walked around the house and enjoyed its soft carpet. He smelled nice things everywhere, overheard snippets of friendly banter, gazed into the blank eyes of different beautiful statues, and began to feel very relaxed. Aeson went down to the cave to look for Han. He was in his lab clicking away on a keyboard that appeared to have been specially designed for his large hands.

"Hey Han," Aeson said, after the door automatically slid open.

"Hi Aeson, you hungry, we usually have dinner all together, but with all the excitement I guess we skipped it. I think Uncle Al stocked your fridge."

"Already ate some sort of fancy wrap. Gourmet food in my own room, crazy."

"Al loves to cook. And he takes requests."

"I might be a different weight class by the time you guys get through with me, but, no I'm not hungry, just wondering if you know what's wrong with my phone?"

Han let Aeson drop the phone into his palm as he tapped on his computer's keyboard with the other hand.

Can we talk later? appeared on his screen.

An answer came back immediately: **See you online** ☺

Han found a cord and plugged it into the fighter's dead phone. It transferred the contents to a bigger screen so that Han could examine its code.

"Looks like a pretty advanced shut-down virus, passed by touch, impressive."

With a few swift key-strokes though the phone lit up with life.

"Thanks!" Aeson said, and immediately checked for texts from his girl-friend.

"No problem. Hey, when you're done, wanna play *Donnybrook*?"

"Is it a fight game?" Aeson asked.

"One of the best I've ever played."

"Then I'm in!"

Chapter 5
FIGHT! FIGHT! FIGHT!

A bowl of apple cores, banana peels, and kiwi skins sat on the couch in between the two passed out gamers. Their faces were hidden within the large diving style oculus masks. It was 4 am in New Jersey and 9 am in London England.

"Wankers fell asleep didya!" shouted a more awake player from Great Britain. He spent all night, and all morning watching and hiding while Aeson and Han incapacitated their mutual enemies along with all of his team mates. Now with no one left and Aeson and Han finally worn out, he was coming out of the woods for digital blood.

"C'mon wankers! Wake it up!" the Englishman's avatar, a plate mail covered knight shouted.

Aeson snored, his physical head hanging from the weight of the Oculus. His avatar, a generic looking guy in denim who had silver hands, also slept, his back against the body of a great tree. The sun was coming up on the game and Aeson's side was not just off guard, they were totally unconscious.

"Wake it up Yanks!" shouted Lionel Stevens from the London flat he shared with four others. He was thirty seven years old and like his mates considered himself an artist. Lionel's medium was the written word. Lately though, all he seemed to be able to write were angry messages to other gamers who happened to fall asleep during one of his bouts of total insomnia.

WANKERS WAKE IT UP! slid across their screens. It was the impolite knight's final attempt to goad them to stand and fight. Clad in medieval armor, the Englishman wielded a large Excalibur style sword. Aeson donned metallic hand wraps to give his punches that extra oomph; only he was snoring. Han used the Monkey King avatar for all his gaming, so he was armored like the knight, and wielded his trademark iron pole, but he was too tired to lift it. With Aeson out Han had lost all motivation to continue. Han sat with his back to the tree as well, and his dreams mingled with the digital stimuli coming through to his eyes and ears.

A "shing!" sound rang out when the angry knight unsheathed his blade. Bludgeons and blades were of course all perfectly legal in *Donnybrook*.

"I told you wankers! Stand and fight, or die like cowards!"

The blade rose and fell in an arc, and finally Han lifted his head. The 3-D weapon coming straight at him was nothing short of menacing and triggered him into alertness. "Wake up Coach! Aeson! The game is still on!"

"What? Go back to sleep dude. Remember training starts today," Aeson groggily stated, not realizing that his face was still encased in the large virtual reality Oculus mask.

The sword's pixels fell, and its coding gave it a sharpness that could remove a player's head.

"Ching!" rang out, just before the broadsword made contact with the slouched and barely conscious duo. Another sword blocked, then another, then a shield, accompanied by a stabbing spear. The knight kneeled uncontrollably after taking someone's spear point right through his armor's armpit.

"Ahhh! Who the bloody devil is playing now!"

"Katya is what I'm known as in here metal head. I'm an ancient Indian goddess and a slayer of crooked knights who kill gamers in their sleep!"

Han woke fully then slapped Aeson's knee. The fighter folded his arms tighter and ignored his new pupil's request.

The avatar's cache of life points began to bleed out. He used a grabbing feature in a last ditch effort, and took hold of Katya's spear shaft after dropping his sword.

"I will surrender to you lady. I don't want to lose this one, been building his life for too long," said Lionel Stevens from beneath his mask. In real life he sat in his boxer shorts, surrounded by fast food wrappers, empty beer bottles, and withered paperback books.

Katya looked down at Han and said, "You were gonna kill my friend."

The Britisher felt fatigue hit him like a cold unforgiving wave. Desperation was clear when he said, "Let me walk and you'll always have a knight to protect you."

"Like I said, you were gonna kill my friend, and that, sir, is unforgivable," Han watched the British knight get run through, scream in utter rage and despair, then disappear, retired from the game *Donnybrook* forever.

"Whoa, Kat, you didn't have to…"

"I know, but it didn't look like your new best friend was going to help."

"Kat, why are you…?"

"Upset? Maybe because my father's a jerk. He came home drunk again and knocked over a lamp. That's why I'm still up."

"Oh, that stinks. You're OK right?"

A long pause made Han squirm a bit in his seat. He felt impatient as he awaited his friend's answer.

"I'm fine. I guess. Your dad is probably cool. He did get you your own private coach," Han could hear Katya say as her avatar stood idly in place, her four arms waving with watery movements.

"It's not like that Kat, my father's not around."

"Well, you never talk about your dad Han, I'm just curious."

"I'm not really allowed to."

"Sorry. One of those situations I guess."

"I guess," said Han.

"You sound tired," Katya, his online friend and *Donnybrook* savior noticed.

"I am. It's 4 in the morning."

"Later then?"

"Later."

———

By five that morning Aeson was in the gym. He went to the mat, dimmed the lights, and warmed up with shadow fighting. After thirty minutes he was loose. He went through his striking routine and thought about Han and what exactly he was being paid to do with him. Hundreds of kicks, punches, elbows, and knees later, Aeson put his hood up and sat in a full split. He heard the door slide open and Han came in. It looked to Aeson as if sleep still had its hold on the kid.

"Uncle Al wants to know what you want for breakfast coach."

"Coach? Yeah that's me, breakfast, anything but fruit, please, no more fruit."

Han smiled widely, passed the news to Al, then crept into his own bed and went back to sleep.

Although only his second day in their home, gathering together at the table already felt familiar.

Aeson looked around at the healthy vegan feast. Only one chair was empty.

"Where's Han?"

"Sleeping," said Grandma, "If he's caught up on homeschool work we let him sleep."

"Oh no," Aeson replied, putting his pomegranate doughnut down, "if he wants to be a fighter he's got to fuel up first thing in the morning."

The family looked at him with surprise.

"Mr. Cadmus, Aeson, our Han wants to learn how to fight, we all want him to get tougher. When he's thirteen he'll have a lot of decisions to make. But a real fighter like you, no, he's more of a thinker."

"Fighters are thinkers Stella."

"I didn't mean that..."

"Any kiwis left?" It was Han, and as always, the mood instantly lifted.

"We kicked ass..."

"Hey!" Stella corrected.

"Asteroids last night coach! Shot them right out of the sky!"

"Yeah we did. We were about to get our heads handed to us though before your friend got there. She one of your homeschool buddies?" Aeson asked, happy to see Han up early.

"Sort of."

"You guys just friends?" Sal asked from behind sunglasses.

"Just friends Uncle Sal," Han quickly replied, with an air of awkwardness that revealed both his age and one of the difficulties that came with his special genetic situation.

Aeson decided to bail him out; "What grade are you in dude?"

"I tested out of all high school math and science already."

"Kid's taking college physics," said Al proudly.

"But he's got a humanities project that he hasn't yet started," reminded Stella.

"It's mainly humanities I have trouble with."

"You mean those are the classes you actually have to try to do well in kid," Al noted.

"Write any love poems lately?" asked Sal as he sipped his Bloody Mary. He liked his vegetables liquefied and mixed with a generous portion of vodka.

At that moment Han's phone rang, signaling an incoming text. It read: **My dad's indoor golfing today, I can use his VIP room!**

Han tried not to look up at the curious faces. He texted back quickly then turned off his ringer. **Cool, see you in there!**

Before too much attention could be put on her child again Stella announced, "Off to work! Han, please at least start the humanities project. Grandma and I need to set up a promo in one of the Morris County shops. You two..." referring to Al and Sal, "I need you to do the same in Paterson."

Sal smirked slightly at Al before he said, "Of course boss."

———

Katie Carouche pulled the blind open to let in the day's first natural light.

"Good morning my love," she whispered. "The sun's coming up. It's going to be strong today, strong enough to burn off any clouds. Can you believe it's March already?" Katie adjusted some of the free standing lights to point directly at her husband as he slept. She set timers for them to go on and off, just in case she had to run, and if Mr. Senga wasn't going to be around.

Katie poured some water for her husband and arranged some powders that would become his breakfast. She did everything she could to help her husband but she knew all her efforts would have small results in comparison to the injection she needed to get from her boss. She adjusted the curtains to let in sun, but also to make it difficult to see inside. Katie fixed little things as her husband slept. She walked around him, examined his straight posture and his peaceful statue like expression. She pressed her lips to his forehead and whispered, "I love you."

———

Han had his track suit on. It was a lot like the ones worn by his mother, both his uncles, and his grandparents. His was yellow though, like the one Bruce Lee had on in Game of Death.

"OK, let's warm up, fifty jumping jacks," Coach Aeson announced. Aeson knew that he could learn a lot about an athlete from how they warmed up.

"Wait," requested Han, "aren't we going to meditate first?"

"Meditate, yeah," Aeson's mind flashed to an old show called Kung Fu that his father used to show him. Aeson remembered the young boy who requested tutelage from a blind monk. "Close your eyes," the fighter told his student, "now picture your worst enemy." Aeson waited, and watched Han perform the task. When Aeson thought that Han had a clear image in his mind's eye he continued, "Now picture yourself leaping in the air, like Superman. You're flying straight towards this guy. You tighten up your fist in mid-flight, your enemy looks you straight in the face before your fist connects and his head explodes in a blast of colors, like fireworks celebrating your birthday."

Aeson observed Han's efforts. The kid's eyes closed tightly, his fists clenched and released, his jaw too, before a celebratory smile etched itself across his face.

"Nice work kid. You can open your eyes now." Han opened them and really seemed more relaxed and ready than ever. "So, who'd you blast? Who'd you knock out, destroy, explode?"

Han's smile became tinted with more than a hint of shame. He spoke with difficulty. "In my meditation... I... leaped in the air like you said, and with all that I had... I... I blasted my dad. Right in his stupid face."

———

Her yellow sport's car pulled into the long, winding driveway. The giant gates sealed her in. She turned her hitting board around and rubbed her red knuckles. She waited for the metal hound to come over and give permission to use the facilities.

"You know why I'm here. I need VIP access."

The room was much bigger than the one Han's uncles helped him build; five times the size in fact. Katie entered the padded, enclosed arena, wearing the head to toe 3-D printed nano tech suit. She stretched, kicked, punched, and rolled in the darkness. She activated her avatar, and then repeated the codes and passwords required to enter the VIP world. A deep, pitch, inky darkness enveloped her.

———

Han's limbs didn't move the way his coach's could. His legs wanted to jump up and down, and not open up too wide. Han's arms didn't flap the way Aeson's did either, they dangled in front of his body and rose over his head, only to come down as if to smash something with both fists.

Coach Aeson knew he had his work cut out. He was going to have to do what his own father had always advocated. It was one of the lessons he had tried to pass on to his son that he had learned from his days in the Marine Corps. He had taught him that when necessary a warrior had to improvise, adapt, and overcome. Aeson had used that lesson to guide himself through success in wrestling, kickboxing, jiu-jitsu, and eventually, when he was of age, MMA. How can I apply my training to this special kid he wondered?

They ended their session with grappling, something that Han's body type was perfect for. The kid was so unbelievably strong and agile Aeson just needed to figure out how harness his power. "Okay. You work on your humanities project like your mom said, and we'll get back to training tonight."

"Got it coach," Han replied, exhilarated from his first lesson. Han's new outlet was so enjoyable he felt like night couldn't come soon enough. Han skipped his homework and found Aeson channel surfing.

After stuffing themselves and watching several movies the two passed out again on the couch. Aeson woke up first and checked his phone. "Tell me you started the homework Han."

"Uhh..." Han said sitting up tall and warily looking around for his mother. "Yeah," he continued with the words "in my head," whispered and barely audible.

They met up again in the gym and had just broken a sweat when Sal walked in.

"Hey, maybe you guys want to move this party to somewhere more exciting? It is Friday night," said Salvatore as he sipped on a cocktail. He held in his other hand what appeared to Aeson as a wet leather coat. Sal lobbed the shiny black pile towards his nephew's coach and said, "Try that on guy."

Han began to bounce with excitement and unzip his track suit jacket, "Really! Sweet! Really Uncle Al? We get to show him already!"

"Of course kid," Uncle Al now responded. "But it's between us. Your mother still don't know about everything, capiche?"

"We're gonna tell her when VIP gets approved by the game review board, I know," Han excitedly acknowledged.

Aeson stepped back in curious confusion, and decided to go with the flow and find out what the kid's enthusiasm was all about.

"Well?" asked Han, "aren't you going to put it on?"

"You're telling me I have to wear that thing?"

"Only if you want to have the most fun you ever had in your life coach!" shouted Han, shirtless and eager to get started.

———

Katya entered the portal and looked around to examine the changes from the last time she was in. The Viking heaven theme had improved and beautiful banners and shields adorned stone walls. Odin as usual was walking around greeting visitors. The games master of the entry port looked as if he had done some redesign to his own avatar. Katya laughed inside at his manufactured regality, remembering how important it was to keep within his good graces.

"Katya!" Odin greeted, "Still going with the four armed goddess I see. You know I'm working with a guy who could help you with a redesign. I'm thinking about a toga for myself, and a thunder bolt."

"No thanks, appreciate it though, but this avatar suits me just fine. I just figured out how to use all the arms at once." Katya began to mesmerize the portal's owner with her movements, using one hand to pass in front of his eyes, two to grasp his wrists and pretend to immobilize him, and one to tickle his belly.

"Hey cut it out," Odin reacted, his double horned helmet wiggling about his head, trying to not giggle from the strange sensation happening in his midsection, "that is my command!"

———

Aeson's new suit didn't fit like a glove, it felt like it was painted on his body. It was as if a thin layer of water was moving around his skin.

"Dat a boy Aeson. And don't forget the final touch," Sal told him as he handed over a pair of virtual goggles.

"Thanks," Aeson replied, "but aren't I supposed to be teaching Han how to fight?"

"Of course coach. That's why we hired you. Once you get the suit thing down, and understand how the room works, you can do some of the kid's training in there. You'll be able to do stuff in the VIP world that you can't do in any gym."

The fighter pondered Sal's words as he accepted the goggles and applied them carefully to his face.

Coach and student stood back to back as Uncle Sal closed the padded door. All went black, then Han said something about a password and a level one access code.

Aeson could not suddenly feel his own body. A moment of terror ensued.

"It's OK coach. Remember now you're in the game, you are a part of the virtual reality. You're not just watching it."

"I can't see, and I feel like I'm going to float away," Aeson reported urgently. Part of him wanted to rip the goggles off and run straight out of the VIP room.

"That's just the suit merging with your chemistry. You'll start to see me in a minute or so."

Aeson closed his eyes and regulated his breathing. When he opened them a different version of the kid he worked for was standing before him. Han at glowed and light flickered around him as he came into view. He was bigger, clad in red armor, but his face, in particular his smile, was recognizable. When Aeson heard, "You OK Coach?" his system started to calm down.

"Reach out your hands Aeson, you can feel in this game."

Aeson extended his hands out and Han placed his weapon in his palms.

"Hold it, feel its weight."

"But... how?" Aeson remarked.

"Nano-sensors, it's all in the code and how the suit communicates with the game."

Aeson was blown away for the second time in 48 hours. He stared at Han who now wore the countenance of an ancient Chinese god, and held an object in his hands that didn't really exist. Or did it?

He wrapped his fingers around it and began to move the metallic pole through the air.

"That's it coach have fun with it. You're much stronger in this world by the way, and virtually nothing here can seriously hurt you."

Aeson held, what at first was a fifty pound object, and began to twirl it like a baton. He passed it around his back, and then over his head. He got so excited that he let it go, and it careened out of his hand. Aeson watched Han leap straight up over his head and snatch it out of mid-air.

"Nice Monkey King! And who's the newbie?" another voice from the virtual ether asked. It was Odin, the creator, and master, of Han's favorite VIP portal.

Aeson followed the voice, and realized that his eyes, and his entire nervous system were still adjusting to this new and veritably limitless world.

It was as if all of reality began to rematerialize, and was recreating itself as a giant meeting hall. The new room appeared much bigger than the padded box he had stepped into with Han. It seemed to be a waiting room of sorts, and characters of various shapes and sizes were meandering about greeting each other.

"What do you think Aeson?" asked the red armored simian warrior who held a metal bar in both his hands.

"Han? Is it still you?" Aeson stepped back and questioned.

"Yes it's me, only I'm wearing my Sun Wukong get-up. In here I'm Monkey King, like when we played *Donnybrook*, only this is, well," he looked himself up and down, "this."

"Welcome warrior!" a towering figure with a flowing beard and double horned helmet told Aeson. He could feel something on his shoulder and realized it was "Odin's" hand.

"A friend of the Monkey King is always welcome in my realm," the Norse god king announced. "Beverage?" The portal owner handed Aeson a chalice. "Don't spill it now," he playfully warned.

Aeson grasped the cap, and at first it felt as if he were trying to hold smoke. The wispy feeling fell away as the cup became more real. First he held it, then he lifted it to his lips. There was no taste, only a sensation of warmth throughout his body. An energizing, good feeling ensued. "It's my finest ale newbie!"

"Holy!" was all Aeson could utter.

"Give the realm's new friend a tour Monkey King, and just shout if you need anything."

Aeson followed Han around, and with each step he could see more. The wooden table seemed to go on forever, and high backed chairs stood like sentinels waiting for more guests to arrive.

They stopped at a door marked EXIT. Aeson watched Han hesitate, then look back towards Odin. Aeson turned and saw that Odin was still watching them, as if they were walking in to some sort of danger. "Everything cool Han?" the fighter asked the kid.

"Of course coach. Sometimes unexpected stuff happens on the way to different rooms that's all."

"Unexpected stuff..." Aeson repeated to himself as he followed the red armored avatar. They stepped through the door and Aeson walked into a black void.

"Put your hands on my shoulders coach. Your eyes will adjust in a few seconds." Aeson followed through the darkness until dim and distant lights began to appear. They walked down the corridor that was only illuminated by the signs that hung above different doorways.

Aeson and Han passed many arched entries, each marked by a glowing neon symbol or word. They walked by a sign that read *Ekusasaizu*. "It means exercise room. VIP is open source, like a wiki, and has programmers from all over the world building new rooms every day. To enter portholes like *Valhalla*, you need permission. Luckily Odin's cool, but a lot of rooms charge, some just don't let you in, and a few you just don't want to enter."

"Interesting." Aeson didn't know what else to say. He had no reference for what he was experiencing. Reality and dreams were mingling. He felt so light, as if he could bounce to the ceiling. He wondered if he would hit his real head on the actual padded roof.

"The high quality avatars, the ones with the best code, will seem more real to you no matter what form they show up in," Han explained.

Beings who appeared as if they had walked in from the ancient past began to materialize before Aeson's perception. A Spartan warrior eyed him through his helmet's mask as he walked by. A geisha girl, with rosy cheeks on top of snow white skin smiled and glided past them, dragging the fighter's stare with her.

"You know that might not even be a woman right? Just saying, most people here are wearing avatars," Han reminded.

"I know that," Aeson replied, secretly glad for Han's admonition. Realizing then that he was subject to the same strange laws of virtual reality, Aeson looked at his hands, and up and down his own body. He was barefoot, and in his most familiar fight shorts.

"It's what you wore in your last fight, so we programmed it into your suit. Clothes aren't considered to be an avatar by the VIP, they're just... virtual clothes. You're traveling as yourself in here, unless you want to choose a new identity," Han informed.

"This works for me. It is me. Anyway, show me more. What else can we do?"

"Sure coach," replied Han. He took a step back, stood straight and attentively, then began a set of perfectly fluid and fully extended jumping jacks. "See, it's like Uncle Al said, we can get a lot done in here."

Aeson watched in wonder and became eager to try his own moves out.

"In here Aeson the intention is just as important as the action," said Han.

Suddenly the fighter felt like he was floating. He wasn't disconnected like when they first entered though, this time the levitation sensation was different. His virtual body was being lifted off the ground. He was yet again perplexed because Monkey King stood in front of him and both his hands were on his weapon. Aeson looked down and began to feel, along with the added elevation, a crushing sensation in his chest. Two arms had wrapped around him from behind and were now attempting to lift and squeeze him.

"Feels like we're about the same weight," a voice sounded off in his ear, "that makes it a fair fight right?"

"Put him down!" Han demanded.

"Or what?" the voice asked, "You gonna tell Odin to banish me?" it continued mockingly.

Aeson surged with confusion, and then something he had not felt since his last fight happened, rage. He was out of his own element, and someone was picking him up as if he were a helpless child; not a good combination of factors for someone who suffered from Immediate Explosive Disorder.

Aeson reacted, and drove his head backwards into the nose of the offending bear hugger.

"That a boy! Sal told me you were tough, and I've watched your fights," he said, but continued to lift Aeson higher. Aeson looked down and watched the ground get further away, he wiggled one arm out and drove his elbow backwards. This time his strike caused the offender to drop him. Aeson fell down and collapsed on legs he still didn't totally understand how to use.

When Aeson turned around, to his utter shock, he saw someone he recognized. Andrew "Guido" Ritigliotti, an MMA fighter from New Jersey who dropped out of the fight scene a few years back. He too was only clad in fight shorts. Both his shoulders bore tattoos of female silhouettes.

"You look like you remember me Cadmus? We never got to tangle, so let's have some fun."

"Not in here Guido!" echoed Odin's voice.

"Let's settle this in *Donnybrook*, I'm with Monkey King and the newbie!" another, female voice, announced.

The four arms of Katyaini, the warrior goddess, each brandished a deadly weapon, and moved them all simultaneously in a menacing display.

Aeson looked around and there must have been three times as many characters mulling now to see what all the commotion was about.

"Forget *Donnybrook* sweet cheeks. And keep that sword in your pants. We're gonna do this like real men. No avatars allowed in the UU room! And there's money to be made."

Aeson noticed that many faces turned from curious to excited. A new door seemed to have appeared behind them and two large neon letters,

UU, glowed above it. A bouncer who was bigger even than Odin stood in front of the entry way. The crowd which was full of characters from all corners of the human imagination began to shout, and then chant in unison. It was the rough song that Aeson first heard in elementary school. It still elicited the same tunnel vision type of response. The words Fight! Fight! Fight! echoed throughout the Tunnel, and a line began to form in front of the menacing and now smiling bouncer.

Chapter 6
BUSTING THE DAM

NO AVATARS ALLOWED read yet another neon sign. Guido looked over at his upcoming opponent and clarified, "Can't get an avatar through if you tried baby! It's all in the coding. That's what the nerds tell me anyway."

Guido's smile grew into a malicious grin as he took hold of and vigorously shook a fierce looking barbarian who happened to be walking by. Guido man-handled the much bigger, much hairier individual, then threw him in between the bouncer's wide stance and right through the saloon style doors.

The easily toppled Conan character was hurled into the UU's red carpet entrance. The barbarian shouted gaming slang in a surprisingly childish voice, "Frickin Mob!" as he fell to the floor and instantly transformed. The ancient warrior was revealed to be a very blubbery little guy who was probably no older than Han.

"Ha!" Guido laughed. "That ain't gonna happen to you Cadmus, is it!"

Han saw what went down and made sure to get quickly away from that door. The bleachers, free seating in the UU VIP, were packed, elbow to elbow with a colorful cast of wandering avatars.

Han, Katya, and Odin all sat together in the bleacher room to watch the apparent fight that suddenly was going to happen. This is why VIP is so cool, Han thought to himself. It's so unpredictable.

Ringside seats cost a lot of VIPcoin and, just like Guido told Aeson, no avatars were permitted. Han was still terrified to show his true self to anyone he wasn't close to. As Katya put one of her four hands on his shoulder, and Odin raised his glass to cheer on Aeson, Han wished that he'd never have to leave the anonymous, free feeling world of the VIP.

———

Uncle Sal turned on the television. After whispering the right words into his phone the Ultimate Underground's logo showed on the screen. He pulled up a stool and instinctively looked over his shoulder. Sal sipped his drink and watched with his chin raised attentively.

"What you watching Sally? And where the hell's Ally?" asked Grandpa Vincent, surprising his son nearly off his bar stool. Vincent was in his 70's and slept a lot, but when he moved his feet were as light as they were when he was still fighting in the ring. Sal changed the channel he was watching a split second before Vincent's eyes could zero in on the screen. Grandpa's curiosity was peaked.

"C'mon, since when you watch house shows?"

"They're interesting Pop, lots of good ideas."

"How many drinks you have? You up to something ain't ya Sally boy?"

"No Pop, just relaxing."

"You're supposed to be in Paterson, setting up the new display for ya sista."

"We got dat covered, you want me to make you a smoothy or something Pop?"

Grandpa ignored his son's question, sensing strongly that something was awry. He walked to the back of the room, through Han's hangout, down the hallway, and stopped beneath the VIP sign. Sal put his Bloody Mary on the bar and followed quickly behind.

Vincent senior was on his tip-toes peering through the very small window when Sal caught up with him. It was dark but he thought he could see his grandson sitting on the floor talking to himself as Aeson jogged in place. Both were clad in skin-tight body suits and wore what looked to be swim goggles.

"What the...?" Vincent whispered.

Sal answered him, "It's a new training device Pop, cutting edge stuff. We got the plans online. C'mon Pop, let 'em train."

Vincent watched in wonder as Aeson walked, jogged, appeared to speak to himself, and periodically came centimeters from bumping into one of the padded walls.

"What the hell's a matter with them?" Vincent questioned.

"Nothing Pop. It's virtual reality. They're in a video game."

Sal begged his father to leave Han's training alone. He put his free arm around Vincent's shoulders and walked him out to the nearest love seat.

The Ultimate Underground was starting on the TV above the bar. Vincent became quickly curious about this virtual world, and asked a series of clarifying questions. "I told you Pop, they're in the video game now. Nobody's getting hurt." Vincent became more curious but tried to put some trust in his youngest child. "Sit back and enjoy the show Pop."

Sal re-seated himself on his barstool. He turned his head quickly when Grandpa screamed, "Take it to him Aeson!" Sal raised his glass to his father, took a sip, then smiled contentedly.

———

Aeson looked around as Guido bounced and raised his arms to commend himself as if he had already won. The ceiling lit up with thousands of stars. "Those are Guido's fans logging in from all over the world," a voice from behind Aeson explained. The fighter turned quickly to find a dwarfish man standing next to an even smaller stool. "And those foggy faces out there, the avatars, they're in the bleachers. I'm your corner man, name's Alviss. First time right? But you've got a few fights on the outside?"

"On the outside? You mean the real world? I've been a pro for over a year little guy," reacted Aeson.

The fighter could feel the small man's hands on his shoulders, and realized that the VIP suit itself was constricting and relaxing around his trapezius muscles. The feeling was so slight that it was barely noticeable. It felt like tiny birds' feet running back and forth.

How would a punch or a kick to the face feel? Aeson's whole face, like Spiderman's, was covered by the nano-suit. His eyes were encased in the digital swim goggles to receive visual stimuli, but the rest of him was wrapped in the tactile nano material.

"Ladies and gentlemen! Welcome back to the Ultimate Underground!" The ceiling twinkled with thousands of fans, and the announcer became illuminated by the growing, virtual, attendees. "Tonight, for some, today for others, we have got quite a live show for you!"

Twinkles filled Aeson's eyepieces and cheers poured out of the Zucharino's wall embedded speakers. The spectral like faces in the bleacher seats seemed otherworldly. Aeson thought he saw a man with a reptilian face, and a woman who appeared made of stone.

"A newbie versus a guido!" the MC shouted.

The cage glowed in a white light, more fans logged on for a few VIP pennies a piece, and the ceiling area above the cage burned with a blinding phosphorescent glow. Guido raised his arms in the happy knowledge that he was making a small percent of all entry fees.

"Everybody loves newbies Aeson!" Guido shouted. "You're good for business!"

"We got fans! We got fighters! Now you've got ten more seconds to place your bets!" shouted the gregarious announcer of the Ultimate Underground.

The MC let go of the mic and it floated in front of him like a pet hummingbird. He raised both his hands and out stretched his fingers. The announcer, clad in a bright blue suit and sporting a high head of shiny hair recoiled one finger at a time as the audience counted down from ten.

"Hey, corner man," Aeson beckoned the dwarf who had started to give him a massage.

"It's Alviss," he corrected.

"Sorry, Alviss, look, I've got to ask, can I... get killed in here?"

"No way, game commission won't approve it because of the money that's being made, but it's actually totally safe... in my opinion. The suit constricts upon impact, but you can't get dismembered or anything like that. Broken bones are practically impossible."

"Newbie!" shouted the announcer, "Are you ready!"

Aeson stood.

"Guido! Are you ready!"

Ritigliotti not only leaped up, but with his jump came a perfectly executed front flip.

"Fight!"

"Yeah, the suit takes a while to master. But you can do all sorts of cool tricks if you know how to guide its energy," the corner man explained quickly.

"Its energy?" Aeson tried to clarify.

"Ding!"

"Yeah, you know, the stuff that makes the world go around."

Round one began, and the lights up top temporarily dimmed.

———

"Han, this is awesome! Your new friend is crazy though!" yelled Katya. The fans all around them were excitedly boisterous and the only way to be heard was to scream. Some of the spectators appeared to be intoxicated, probably on homemade geek drugs, sitting in the safety of private VIP rooms. They were cutting loose and partying in their own antisocial way.

"Who's your money on, Monkey Boy?" asked a slurred voice that came out of a generic looking superhero avatar. His red cape was programmed to blow in a permanent breeze.

Han tried to ignore the drunken super guy behind him, but Katya couldn't. She stood up, her hands touching the hilts of various weapons. Odin turned to her and said, "Easy Katya. Edged weapons don't do anything anyway in here, and could get us kicked out."

"Fine," she responded. The superhero swayed ever so slightly and stared at her amusedly. Katya shouted, "It's Monkey King! Loser!" and fired a quick straight punch to his lettered chest. The boozy superhero was sent rolling backwards from the well practiced shot.

When security showed up Katya simply pointed at the caped crusader and said, "I thought you guys were cracking down on drunks in here?"

———

The suit squeezed where the virtual foot hit it. The first blow was to Aeson's arm. Normally he'd have used this block to set up his right cross, but virtual Guido was too quick, and way too experienced for Aeson.

The fighter realized in that moment that there were many worlds, that he was still in a padded, box shaped room fighting the air, and Guido was somewhere doing the same. There was the world of code where they both fought each other in, then there were the viewers, watching images that the suit's data produced. There were thousands of lights, so there were thousands of fans, logging in to phones and TVs from trains, bars, living rooms, and street corners. Aeson remembered depressingly the sparse audiences that turned out for even his biggest fights.

Guido used a fighting technique that would have been impossible in the non-virtual world, and showed off his status to the fans as a VIP veteran.

"Agghh!" Aeson heard himself gasp in frustration, as did real Han, who sat on the floor in the corner of the VIP room, feeling as if he let his new coach fall unprepared into a bad situation.

———

Monkey King jumped as if his seat were on fire, worried that his coach was already losing.

How did he get me over his head? the fighter thought, just before he was thrown down onto the comic book blue canvas.

Grandpa Vincent pulled himself away from the screen and out of the loveseat as Aeson was being held aloft. He ran to Han's hangout. Sal didn't bother to get in his father's way. He remembered how startled he was by this new technology when he first saw it in action.

Gazing through the small window again Grandpa Vincent watched the actual Aeson lose his balance and his grandson Han cringe in worry. To Vincent they were acting like deranged mimes in skin tight suits, performing a skit that no one seemed to see. But he could see him on the TV! Vincent made sure to exhale, like he used to do when he got nervous before a fight.

Sal watched the crowd go wild. Aeson looked upwards in the game world and could see thousands of new lights logging on. His gaming body was lifted higher before it was hurled back downward. The fighter fell with a crash in the virtual world, and bounced off the canvas before crumbling in a heap. In the Zucharino's studio he collapsed as if he were a puppet whose strings were cut in one swoop.

Guido stood over him and taunted with both hands, "Get up! You're a pro right! Show me! Show them what you got!"

Aeson kipped up in the padded room. Grandpa scurried back to the TV to see what Aeson's efforts were going to accomplish in this crazy new world.

The fighter's next move caused his virtual self to become aerial and Aeson was surprised at how high his jump seemed to take him. Guido knew what to do, and used his round-house kick to knock him right out of the sky. The fighter smashed against the virtual fences and gritted his teeth in utter rage. He looked up to see his opponent moving in for another spectacular lift.

Aeson instinctively tackled. Guido took his momentum, and instead of falling and getting ground and pounded he stutter stepped backwards, hooked his arms over Aeson's back and around his waist, and looked up to the fans for approval as he bent backwards to take the fighter out of his crouch and back into the air.

The fighter was in shock, to be lifted a second time was unbelievable, but now to be held upside down, as if he were a total weakling, simply humiliated him.

Han screamed for his coach to go with it, and "Land on your feet!"

Within the matted New Jersey gaming room Aeson's back bent backwards as if he was possessed by a demon.

Vincent screamed at the TV, "Break his grip kid!"

Sal laughed and checked his phone for betting statistics.

In the UU Aeson came down right on top of his head. The suit pinched his neck slightly, but he knew if Guido were to have done that to him in real life he'd be dead. The lights above were absolutely blinding. He could not match Guido's virtual savvy. There seemed no way to win.

"Settle down Aeson," the corner man told him as he applied an icy compress to Aeson's neck. "Remember, every movement sends out data. Move too fast and your data loses its balance."

"What?" the fighter questioned with frustration. Aeson wanted the advice to end because thinking got in the way of his fighting. It was too late to strategize, he thought, time to kill or be killed, virtual or not.

"Just stay on your feet. Less is more," the corner man encouraged reluctantly, for Aeson's face appeared to harbor the almost pleasured expression of a warrior demon.

Sal checked his phone, the odds against Aeson were even higher than he expected. He slurped the last of his cocktail down.

Round two started and Aeson stood up slowly, his fists in front of him as if he were protecting himself in the dark, oblivious to what was coming next. Guido spun on one foot then approached his opponent cockily and with his hands down.

Aeson's utter rage was focused, and suddenly the lights were gone, and the ghostly faces disappeared. It was happening, and it was happening now. The doctors called it Immediate Explosive Disorder, and shame followed with the diagnosis; as did counseling, and prescription pills. When it was happening though, it was awesome, after all, it was a fight, and to Aeson, the rage felt like it was supposed to be there. There was only Andrew the Guido Rittigliotti in front of him. And he was going down. Aeson crouched, like a panther readying itself. He leaped, going against his corner's recommendations, and became like a firework with a quick burning fuse. To Guido's delight Aeson shot passed him and was on a collision course with the roof of the cage. He looked up and laughed out loud. Then, when he realized what Aeson was doing, Guido froze.

The leaping contender flipped in mid air and pushed off of the digital boundary. Aeson's Superman punch was now reversed, and his fist was aimed straight for Guido's crown.

The impact created a whiplash motion in Guido's neck, and, his smile gone, made him stumble drunkenly. Aeson rolled to his feet and fixed his glare on his opponent.

"I told you!" Han shouted.

"Right again kid," said Odin, "I mean... Monkey King."

"Walk in slow Aeson, stay low, steady... Hit him Aeson!" Vincent barked toward the TV.

The fighter stepped forward carefully and unleashed a furious combination of punches just as Guido turned to face him. As if it were choreographed Guido dodged each blow, then finished the routine by sending Aeson flying backwards with a front kick to the midsection. Aeson was stunned and shocked that he had so easily gone down, but getting kicked felt great to him, this was no video game anymore. "Absorb his shots Aeson," his corner man told him, "and push back with small movements as he hits you."

The fighter nodded, a part of him fearful of his own rage, and tried to normalize himself. He stood back up, only to receive a knee to the face. The fighter stumbled and found himself down again. Things his corner man shouted made sense in theory but Aeson couldn't apply them. He looked around as Guido slowly moved in for the kill, and thought he could see Han, and a bunch of other fantastical looking avatars staring down and shouting at him. As he began to stand, knowing that Guido was going to find a way to cold cock him, he heard another voice, it was familiar but sounded as if it were coming from inside his head.

"Stand slow kid, and with your hands up! You can take this guy!" It was Han's grandfather's voice. Vincent was hurling commands through the closed padded door. "That's it, keep your eyes on this bastard and your dukes up! Be his punching bag for a minute, you got nothing to lose!"

OK Grandpa Vincent, I hear you, Aeson thought, why not? The fighter smiled. He stood up slow and steady. Vincent watched him rise as he directed, his fists up, his muscles clenching every time a blow was struck. With every shot he took his berserker battery became more charged.

"Now slow jabs, pepper this guy and keep your chin down!"

Aeson began to pump out medium speed left jabs, despite getting hit with roundhouse kicks to his thighs and hooks to his body. Guido raised both his hands and dodged each one of Aeson's attacks while hitting him and egging the audience on. "What's next big man!"

"Now Aeson, blast him with the overhand hand right and don't stop hitting until he taps! Hold da back of his head wit your left and keep slamming him with your right!" Dirty boxing, Aeson thought, I like it.

Vincent scurried back to the bar TV as fast as he could, only to watch Aeson execute his plan to a tee.

Aeson's focus did not waiver and his intent became nothing short of murderous.

"Dude, your guy's taking it to him now," said Katya, her observation imbued with awe.

"He sure is!" yelled Odin, as he slapped Han on his armored back cheerfully.

Many of the fans were shocked at the newbie's recovery turned blitzkrieg. Soon surprise turned to anger as many audience members realized they were losing their bets. Some cheered anyway, as Aeson's fists were thrown like machine gun fire, and the cocky Guido could do nothing but take it.

Before round 2 ended the fighter Aeson Cadmus had Guido pressed up against the cage. Aeson realized, in this virtual world, not only could focused relentless striking work to your advantage, but wrestling, with a slow steady but full force pressure, could turn the tides towards victory. Aeson's face nearly touched his opponents as he dug in with his feet and pushed, all the while seemingly frozen in mid-step within the padded VIP room.

Within his goggled perspective the fighter saw the sweat dripping from Guido's brow. Aeson's face heated up as the energy of his opponents breath pushed out against millions of nano-particle fibers in his own mask.

Aeson could feel Guido's body pushing back and decided to try what his own father had called Busting The Dam. Keep the pressure on your opponent, and get them to pressure back as hard as they can. At the last possible second, before the buildup of energy bursts, bust the dam by moving out of the way. As your opponent releases, with no ability to stop, you catch him in a choke hold.

Han screamed, "Yeeeee!" and proudly bared his teeth in excitement. Odin stood up too and raised his chalice shouting "Victory!"

Once the fighter's guillotine choke was locked into place, he was not about to let go. There was one minute left on the round's clock and Aeson was going to use every second of it to squeeze his opponent unconscious. If the suit can constrict, Aeson thought, then I can choke this guy out. I'm going to squeeze until it feels like this guy's head is going to pop off, and in here nobody's gonna stop me, or fine me for letting it all out. That's the way dad taught me to fight.

Sure enough, with twenty seconds still left on the clock, Aeson could feel a rhythmic, but frantic percussion on the side of his thigh. Andrew the Guido Rittigliotti had tapped out. Aeson the Fighter Cadmus had secured his first Ultimate Underground victory.

Chapter 7
VIP COIN

There were no avatars allowed in the Ultimate Underground, but Aeson had a hard time believing that the announcer was his real self. His bright mauve suit was certainly programmed, but how could one be born with such a face? Bradley Bestial appeared to have eyes like a shark, the long toothy grin of a hyena, with a thin pointy nose that seemed to be growing towards his mouth. Bestial's sweat seemed tangible, and his high doo-wop hair was shiny with moisture.

"The champ undone! The Fighter emerges! Aeson Cadmus is number one! Beginners luck or are you the real deal!"

The fighter looked around, huffing and puffing. The rush of adrenaline that rose in him during the fight gradually gave way to a flood of endorphins. A feeling of sweet relief coursed beneath his skin.

"I didn't know this was a championship fight, but I'm glad I rallied," Aeson spoke into the mic.

"Championship he says?" Bestial stretched over and asked. "Ladies and gentlemen, Aeson Cadmus is a newbie!"

The audiences burst into uproarious laughter.

"You're a dead man Cadmus!" screamed Guido as two bouncers formed a wall of muscle to block him.

"You hear that Cadmus! Guido wants a rematch!" yelled Shark Eyes.

"He ain't even contracted Brad! Tonight's purse should still go to me!" Guido shouted.

Aeson hadn't even known that virtual fighters could get paid. One minute he was exploring Han's video game scene, the next minute he was back in the cage, with more fans watching him fight than ever before.

"You hear that Cadmus, you need a contract, collateral for the UU to let you fight here. We got any takers!" Bestial cried as he waved his Caesar like hand towards the distant twinkling audiences. A woman was suddenly opening the gate to the cage. She walked straight past the bouncers, in fact they stepped out of her way. Her tight white gown accentuated her tan skin and curvy figure. Slight pressure moved over Aeson's shoulders before the feeling of a wet plum pressed itself against his lips. "What's a matter sweetie, never been kissed in the VIP world?"

Aeson stared into her blue eyes and could see so much more than eyeballs staring back at him. He saw himself wearing a championship belt while straddling a magnificent motorcycle; the type of bike only someone with a lot of extra cash could by. His own face looked relaxed because his financial worries were over. He was smiling at the world. But who was this woman? And where was Lenora?

Quicker than she had arrived she was gone. In fact everything disappeared. Aeson knew only that he was puckering up in a padded room and wearing a now slimy skin tight garment.

"Game over kid," said Sal. The wider he opened the door the more Aeson could experience the enjoyment of room temperature air. "Before you do anything stupid we should talk. And drink some water. Everybody forgets how thirsty the box makes you."

"That was awesome!" shouted Han as he ran on all fours out of the steamy sensor filled cauldron.

"Posture," reminded Vincent, which made Han stand up completely straight.

"Sorry Grandpa," said Han as he rummaged through the bar's fridge looking for coconut waters.

"Aeson, catch!"

Aeson caught the boxed drink and took in Han's smiling image. What's it like to be him, he wondered again, and how did he get this way? Before Aeson could debrief and celebrate with the kid Sal laid out some guidelines. "Han's mother can't know 'bout this yet. VIP is a learning tool; no such thing as Ultimate Underground. Capiche? Grandpa knows now but ain't gonna tell anybody. Whenever you get out of the room take a shower, those suits are starting to stink already. Wear them in with you. It's the best way to get 'em off anyways. And three. I bet money for you, on you. You made almost 30 VIPcoin off that fight Aeson, and ya haven't even got a contract yet. Wit a contract you would a made anywhere between 40 and 45 VIPcoin before bets were even in."

"Okay..." answered Aeson, confused but optimistic, most curious about the final bit of information Han's uncle told him.

As he walked upstairs Grandpa Vincent grabbed his hand and shook it hard, "Nice work guy. You really let him have it."

Aeson remembered the voice in his head, and the good corner advice Vincent had given him through the door. "Thanks for your help Vincent, I felt like a fish outta water in there."

"But you did good. And earned some of those new coins," replied Vincent before sitting down again, and smiling contentedly.

"How much is that worth in real money anyway?" asked the fighter.

"Beats me kid, ask my grandson."

"About $10,000," Han responded, "If you do a straight conversion," sipping his drink and standing up exaggeratedly straight, "worth a lot more on the open underground market of course."

Aeson's eyes stretched wide when he heard Han's answer and suddenly he had more questions about this strange new virtual arena.

"Take a showah guy! We'll talk numbers when you're clean," said Sal after putting a fresh celery stick in a brand new cocktail.

———

"Dammit! His fat uncle did it again!" shouted Katya when she realized Han was offline and she was still waiting in the bleachers.

"Easy Katya, he's twelve, he's not in charge of his VIP room," said Odin.

"Whatever... I'm the same age as him and I don't just pop out without even saying goodbye."

"You're twelve?"

"I've got to go. See you in *Valhalla*."

Katie Carouche stood in the shower and cried. It was the only place she allowed herself to break down. As she turned off the water, the black pile of nano-suit at her feet, she sensed a presence. It was the robot dog, and it was pushing the bathroom door open.

"I know you are working hard to acquire information about the boy," an electronic voice spoke through the robot's speakers, "from what you've told me he seems healthy, and stable, is that correct?"

She made a circle on the glass door to see the creature who was communicating with her and responded, "Yes. He shows no sign of ill health."

"I need more though. I need you to prepare him for our eventual meeting."

"How?"

"You need to let him know the truth; that I disappeared for his safety."

"If I tell him that will you treat my husband?"

"Not without results. I need my son, and he deserves the truth."

"The truth! That will blow everything! He'll never believe any of that and won't trust me anymore!"

The robot inched forward and revealed something in its mouth. "This is an eighth of a dose and it will sustain your partner temporarily. It is incentive for what you must do."

Without toweling off Carouche stepped through the steam and grabbed for the syringe.

"Thank you," she said, with a reluctance that bordered on sounding ungrateful.

"Just do the job, convince him that his father is not the monster he thinks he is."

Carouche dropped the sopping wet VIP suit on top of the dog as she exited the bathroom. She dressed quickly and never let the formula out of her hand.

———

Lenora's text message to Aeson read, **Everything going OK?**

With his shirt not fully on he texted back, **Great!**

"Yo Aeson! I don't want to miss the brunch special guy," warned Sal from behind his bedroom door.

Talk later you're not going to believe it! typed Aeson excitedly.

Okay? was Lenora's dissatisfied but hopeful response.

Love you! Aeson wished he could scream it, but he had to go, Sal was waiting.

Love you too.

Snow was melting when they walked out. The noon sun was bright and steam was rising off the ground. The home's gutters sang with the rush of water.

"Wait Sal," Aeson said as he came to a halt.

"What's up guy?"

"Are we going to be back for Han's afternoon training session?"

"Yeah, sure. He's with his grandpa now, and he's gotta finish his humanities homework. Let's talk business."

———

When Katie Carouche turned the key in the door Mr. Senga was waiting for her.

"How is he?"

Mr. Senga bowed and responded with a question, "Did you acquire the treatment?"

She lost the etiquette she usually used around the soft spoken older Japanese man and pushed past him saying, "I'm sorry, I only have a little..."

Senga kept his hands at his sides and pivoted on one foot as if he were a door smoothly opening. He moved quickly and quietly behind the woman who came to him for help. Senga felt honored to be called upon to assist the wife of one of his best students.

Katie was standing over her husband, holding the syringe, and trembling.

"Please... Kay-tee, let me. I have much experience with this."

She swallowed and was surprised by how much of a comfort the old man was, and what a relief his words were.

"Really? What don't you know how to do well?" she said, handing him her husband's gene therapy injection.

"Many things."

"Well, thanks, here, you do it, please, I'd rather hold his hand as he comes to."

"Hai," said Mr. Senga outstretching his cupped hands to receive the medicine.

She dimmed the lights that shone directly over her husband then kneeled. His fingers were soft to the touch but hard when she squeezed. "Majstro," she whispered, "Mr. Senga's here. We have some of your treatment. You don't need to be scared, you're just going to wake up for a little while." He looked as if he were smiling, just a little smile, as if he knew she was saving him, and would do anything in her power to bring him back completely.

Little holes opened under his nose, his nostrils were returning. Maj's body began to absorb oxygen almost immediately, but it was the first time in two weeks. His degeneration without the treatment had been rapid, and the last thing to go was his mammalian reflex. His body had become more plant than animal, and he began to quite successfully absorb carbon dioxide as a nutrient. Katie squeezed again after hearing the air enter his reawakened lungs and waited. His green, hairless body, began to circulate blood, and she could see veins pulse in his neck. "Vivi, Majstro, my love. Vivi."

She beckoned him to live in the language he had become most comfortable with, and his eyes began to move beneath their lids. Her hand felt slight pressure, enough to cause her to finally smile. She looked up towards Mr. Senga as she spoke to Maj; "I'm going to get the rest of your treatment honey. Don't worry. Just breathe, and know that I love you."

———

The Fort Lee diner sang with the sounds of stacked trays, friendly enough staff, and overworked coffee-machines. The two were lucky to get a booth, and when they finally settled in Aeson felt exhausted.

"Coffee sweet-heart, and juice for my man here," Sal told the young attractive server who wore her hair up in a bun and sported digital eyeglasses. One lens seemed to be active, and danced with small streams of rainbow colors. Aeson looked at her out of curiosity then looked away. The fighter realized that he was the odd one because of his lack of tech exposure. But had she ever been in a VIP room?

"Actually, I'll have coffee too please," Aeson interjected.

"Only one java sweetie," Sal reminded as he put a five dollar bill in the waitress's hand. "Would you prefer VIPcoin?" Sal whispered, his hand not yet off of the five.

To Aeson's surprise she let go and answered, "VIPcoin all the way dude, just bump on my glasses."

She bent over, smiled at Aeson, and allowed Sal to touch his phone to the corner of her spectacles; "Right on man, anything you gents need just ask for Eva."

Sal raised his eyebrows mischievously at Aeson.

"One coffee one juice," she said. Eva adjusted her glasses and looked straight at the fighter, "Sorry big guy, whoever's paying is the one I listen to," she apologized.

As she walked away Sal explained, "The VIP takes more out of you then you think, keep hydrating. Besides, you're in training now; if you want the contract that is."

"I've never even heard of VIP before I met you guys, and now you're telling me the game has its own money?"

"Dat's right kid, you been in those mountains so long you missing all the opportunities of the new world. Course she wants VIP coin. It's independent, unregulated, and just plain cool."

"If I'm going to go into any contractual financial arrangement with you, then I'm going to need you to be a little more open and upfront."

"Shoot. What's on your mind? Seriously," Sal invited.

"Well, let's start with Han, your nephew. He's…"

"He's what Aeson? A kid who is getting ready for a possible big shift in his life, a kid who wants to learn how to fight cuz when he does eventually get out in the world he's probably gonna have to."

"I don't understand. What is this shift? And why can't he leave the house?"

"First off, you're a smart guy, you should know by now people who are different are treated different. People panic, give in to fear when they can't understand things. When Han was born there were some who thought he was a miracle, but others, dangerous nut jobs, who thought he was something else."

"Geez, he's a great kid, if only they could see past, you know, looks."

"Yeah right. My brother and I moved in soon after the kid was born. After a few close calls we decided it was the right thing to do, protect the kid, our nephew. Outsiders just leak stories, pictures, stuff like that; anything to make a buck."

"So what's this shift? He getting Bar Mitsvahed or something like that?"

"No Aeson. He ain't getting Bar Mitsvahed. At thirteen Han's biological father gets to decide whether to file for joint custody or not."

"Who's his father?"

"Guy's name is Jason Badgley as far as I know. Real creep. A straight up egg head scientist. My sistah Stella always liked smart guys."

"He… did something to Han?"

"You think? Maybe, just maybe he did a little something to his genetic make-up?" Sal answered sarcastically, making Aeson not want to ask another question.

Aeson just nodded his head and was thankful when his juice arrived; not only to slake his thirst, but to give him a second to think about all that Sal was filling him in on.

"Now I got a question for you Aeson."

"Alright. What's up?"

"We aksed you this before, but do you know this broad? And why was she in our home?" Sal asked while pushing his phone towards Aeson with an open photo of a woman with short blonde hair.

"Maybe…"

"How 'bout her car?"

Once Aeson saw the yellow sport's car a shiver of cold crawled up his spine.

"Yeah Sal. That must be the woman who gave me a ride before the interview and then dropped me off in Newark."

"And you never met, or even spoke with her before coming to Jersey?"

Another voice drove its way in, along with his large body. "Move over big guy, Ally boy coming through." It was Sal's brother, and Han's other uncle Alexander. "Yeah, as I suspected. Still can't believe she got in the house. We're getting sloppy Sally."

"No Al, you got sloppy," reminded Sal.

"Not even Joe Joe in the precinct could get anything on her."

"And that should'a been your first clue genius."

"Anyways…" Al said, turning slightly towards Aeson and squishing him a little farther into the corner, "you got anything on this broad, or did she find you?"

"She found me, offered me a ride and I took it."

The large boned brothers looked at each other and something unspoken was communicated. Aeson wondered how it all fit together as he drank the rest of his juice down.

"So how'd she know about Aeson?" whispered Al to Sal. Silence ensued. Aeson wanted more juice.

"Moving on," said Sal to Aeson, "VIP is new, Ultimate Underground is new, you got all the stats to make it big in this world. Sign on with us and we take the risks, but you make the profit."

"What do you mean I got the stats Sal? I'm a cage fighter and I'm good."

"Sorry guy," said Al. "We know all 'bout your suspension. Ultra violence is frowned upon now. The new regulations are getting rid of head bangers like you. You're like our father used to be. If you could even pay those ridiculous fines, who's gonna give you a fight? Nobody wants that kind of press guy."

Aeson slammed his empty glass down unconsciously and wanted to squeeze it until it exploded. He barely finished high school, and even if he did go to college or get job training there was nothing he wanted to do except fight. To hear these two men, who sounded like they knew what they were talking about, was life shattering.

"Good thing is Aeson, the UU rewards the kind of rage you got. In the VIP room you got to give it everything just to make an opponent feel your punch. You got what the UU wants, and everybody wants VIPcoin."

"Sounds interesting, but... I don't know. Didn't you guys hire me to coach your nephew? It can't be a ..." Aeson said but stopped because he couldn't think of the word that would fit best.

"A ruse," answered Al. "Absolutely not. Our first priority has always been the kid. Like we said, he picked ya, we're just taking a good situation and making it better."

"A lot better," said Sal. "Give me your phone guy," Sal continued. He took it and slid it towards Al, "Bump him bro. It's time he got his take right. Fair is fair."

Al pinched his own nose, took out his phone, and did what his brother requested.

"Take a look at your new icon guy."

VIP was now there, where it wasn't before, and when he clicked on it his name, along with 30 in the checking column showed up.

"You just gave me ten grand for winning that video game?"

"No! Ten grand can't get you what VIPcoin can." At that moment the waitress returned.

"Gentlemen, another guest has arrived I see, and somebody looks like they just got probed by aliens."

"Not quite sweetie, Aeson over here is a fighter, in the UU, and he just scored his first purse."

"Nice work big guy. The UU is sick! And a VIPcoin goes a long way, especially in the city. I get off work in two hours," she said smiling and nudged Sal's shoulder with her hip. Al bumped Aeson with his elbow, and Sal gave Al a view of the bottom of his chin. The waitress's left eyeglass lens swirled in a multicolor fractal, the sun began to burst through the window and shine onto Aeson's phone, the fighter started a quick climb out of fear and paranoia and began to feel real excited about things again.

———

You going in today?

I don't know. I have a workout with my coach later.

He's out?

Yeah, my uncle and him are talking about stuff.

And they left you alone?

I'm never actually alone.

Let me get in touch later, OK?

Sure.

Katie closed her laptop screen and began to pack some things into a small bag. Mr. Senga stopped at her door.

"You are going somewhere?"

"Yes. Back to New Jersey. It's time I take things into my own hands."

Senga smiled softly. "Perhaps you will need these." He held out the keys to his old Chinook camper and said, "There are many of your husband's things inside it. Perhaps, they may come in handy."

Of course, Katie Carouche thought, my car stands out, and I don't want to be recognized.

"Thank you Mr. Senga. I will not let you, or my husband down."

Chapter 8
MEGA MALLS AND PETTING ZOOS

Han wrote computer code to pass the time. He gave his coach Aeson a few more VIP clothing options and himself a tail. He had studied ancient civilizations in his on-line humanities class and learned about both Hanuman from India and Sun Wukong from China. Both deities were known as the Monkey King. They had tails because unlike him they were hybrid monkeys, made that way by spiritual means, while he was a hybrid ape, created through science; Bonobo ape to be exact. Bonobos share 98.7% of their genetic makeup with human beings, Han shared over 99%.

How did he get this way? Well, that goes back to his father, Dr. Jason Badgley, but it really goes back to 1910, Ilya Ivanovich Ivanov, and the World Council of Zoologists. Ivanov presented his findings and his goals to the council, and by the 1920's he was experimenting with breeding humans and chimpanzees together through artificial insemination. It was all under the brutal and watchful eyes of Joseph Stalin, Soviet Dictator, master manipulator, and provocateur of terror. Why did Stalin want human-ape hybrids? Soldiers of course; strong, obedient, violent when necessary, super soldiers.

Han didn't like to think about this type of stuff. He wanted to be normal, to hang out with other kids, maybe even have a girlfriend.

For now he was stuck in a large house, with a humanities project due, and only his sleeping grandfather to keep him company. He was not like anybody else he'd ever known, or even anyone he'd ever heard of. Han Zucharino was one of a kind, and he felt the loneliness of his status every day. Ivanov never succeeded in his humanzee experiments but somehow Dr. Jason Badgley, Han's father, prevailed with bonobo human hybridization.

Aeson Cadmus was going to teach Han how to be more comfortable with his own unique self, by teaching him how to effectively defend himself. That was why his mom had agreed to hiring a personal martial arts coach. So far he just knew that Aeson was fun to hang out with, and that it was cool having a real MMA fighter sleeping in his house.

Vincent was snoring in his chair when Han came down the stairs, so he decided to put off his humanities homework for one more day and fire up the VIP room by himself.

———

"We want you to think about the ten fight contract guy, and not to make any hasty decisions. You're name's already starting to buzz online," said Sal.

"Today however, we also want you to experience something that the small mountain town yuz came from simply does not have."

"What's that?" asked Aeson, hoping that the two brothers were not about to cross some sort of ethical line.

Sal answered, "Jersey's biggest mega mall."

Al stated, "We got to make a quick run to Patterson, while you get the time to walk around, explore, and make a decision 'bout your future. You might want to give your girl a call. She'll be happy those fines are gonna get paid."

To get to the mall's entrance Sal weaved in and out of cars as if he were the one in a video game. Someone who beat him to an empty parking spot was flipped off, threatened with a lawsuit, and then even asked if he knew who Aeson Cadmus was, cuz he's in this car and if you don't turn around he's gonna kick your ass! Aeson was getting a kick out of Sal's free spirited ways and even started to respect his aggressive, over-the-top mannerisms; "It's what you gotta do when you live here Aeson, else yuz get no respect."

"So how am I supposed to get back Sal?"

"Keep your phone on guy, we'll call ya."

Aeson watched Sal drive away from the five floor supposed shopper's paradise. There was a cool breeze, and haze filled sun beams reflected off of black puddles. Aeson hoped that he would not have to spend much time looking for a magazine store. He already ate, and he completely hated shopping. He didn't like to look at the latest clothes, or electronics, or even apps for his phone. Aeson Cadmus preferred it whenever his girlfriend shopped for him actually. In his mind the necessities were simple - food to eat, a roof to sleep under, and a gym to train in. He was getting all of these at his new job so, basically, a giant super store was the last place he wanted to be.

The mall was a mini city, with five levels of consumer attractions. Aeson decided right away that he would read the latest fight magazines without having to buy them, and then get a gift he could send to Lenora. The virtual woman who kissed him in the Ultimate Underground, although it was out of his control, made him feel guilty; the incident also made him think more about his girlfriend and how much he appreciated her authenticity. The first sale item he saw when he walked in however stopped him dead in his tracks.

"It's a beauty right!" said an apparent saleswoman. "You're welcomed to hop on. It's a Fuel-cell vehicle, zero emissions, switches to electric as well."

"Wow," Aeson heard himself say, the motorcycle was like something he'd seen in a movie. It was sleek but strong, fast but burly, and totally high tech.

"Every emergency feature you can think of sir," the saleswoman, with short black hair, tight leather-like clothing, and fingernails that looked as if they could skewer one of Grandma Zucharino's famous vegan meatballs said as she placed her open palm over Aeson's heart. Her hand was cold and had a synthetic feel to it, even through his shirt. "This bike will never let you fall off. Please, feel free to ride it around the store. There are no harmful emissions, only water vapor. We can pre-set its max speed and activate all hazard sensors."

"Thanks," Aeson responded, trying not to look at the attractive mall worker, just the bike. "I think I should go now... maybe I'll come back later."

The lady moved her hand to his shoulder and stared into Aeson's eyes, "Every emergency feature you can think of sir. This bike will never let you fall off. Please, feel free to ride it around the store. Please, feel free to ride it around the store. There are no harmful emissions, only water vapor. We can pre-set its max speed and activate all hazard sensors." That's weird Aeson thought, she's saying the exact same thing she did five seconds ago and in the exact same way.

"She's a robot, dude," an informative, eager yet tired voice rose up from behind him to say. "Don't be freaked out, please. I have to tell people this. We've had guys ask her out, only to realize, well, she's a machine."

"No," Aeson began to explain himself.

"It's cool dude. Look, the fact is, the type of woman Molly over here represents is the woman who would love to go for a ride on a bike like this one. It's so fricking safe! Climate change beware! If it snows it's got grabbers, if it's 110 in the shade, thing pulls any moisture from the air and sucks it into the jacket and pants that it comes with. Anybody tries to steal it, forget about it. This baby's got a surprise."

Molly looked at Aeson seductively and repeated, "A surprise."

Aeson was officially freaked out by the android and suddenly just wanted to get away and buy something for Lenora; even before looking at fight magazines.

"Best part about this baby..."

"Let me guess," Aeson said, borrowing a little bit of the moxie that Al and Sal Zucharino always threw around, "the price."

"Exactly! We do really easy payment plans and…"

Aeson decided to play now. He knew he wasn't going to drive away with a new motorcycle so he decided to try and have some fun.

"What makes you think I need a payment plan?"

"Best part about this baby…" the android repeated, now throwing in a wink that made Aeson almost take a step back.

"Quiet Molly," the hunched over manager told the sales machine authoritatively, "It's not that I think you need a payment plan sir, it's something we offer to all prospective buyers."

"Prospective buyers," she continued, now putting both her hands on the manager's shoulders, and giving Aeson the creepy feeling that the android was more to him than an unpaid employee.

The out of shape, fatigued, and now irritated manager shrugged Molly off and tried to take control of the situation.

"Look, it's cool, if you don't have the money, the bicycle store is down at the other end of the mall, "maybe they have something with training wheels that you would like."

"Training wheels…" Molly repeated. All three stared at each other and Aeson had the impulse to fight back but decided against it. Instead he pulled away and said, "It's a nice bike, but you guys probably don't take VIPcoin anyway."

"Molly, take a break OK. This customer and I are going to talk privately."

"Taking a break," she responded, and with a mechanical sway to her hips, walked away.

"You give me fifteen VIP coin for this baby right now, I'll buy the bike with my discount and give it to you in exchange."

"Whoa… slow down guy," Aeson heard himself say in his best Sal Zucharino impersonation, "I think I need something with training wheels instead." Aeson waved to the android, "Bye sweetheart, you're doing a great job."

The fighter checked his phone as he walked away. He saw his small reflection and realized he was smiling.

———

VALHALLA CLOSED read the sign. That stinks, Han thought to himself, I guess Odin is finally taking a break.

Without the familiar porthole which Han had a permanent guest pass to because he had made friends with the owner he would be forced to walk the VIP's open access platform delivery system, the Tunnel. This access route was not preferred by virtual visitors, and fear of it in fact kept many gamers away. The VIP's *Tunnel* was the definition of unregulated, and unsavory things often went unpoliced. When Uncles Sal and Al built the VIP for Han they made him promise that he would never walk the *Tunnel* without a group, but nobody was around, and Han, quite frankly, was sick of being treated like a baby. The *Tunnel* was totally safe, Han tried to convince himself, if not for identity thieves, child pornographers, and actual terrorists.

"Armor!" he called out for and was granted. "Weapon!" done. "Tail!" All were his. He transferred his only VIPcoin into his avatar's account. His uncles always told him to have a little something, just in case. He texted Katya to let her know his plans, but she said she would be otherwise occupied most of the day.

The padded door closed and he slipped the final piece of his suit over his eyes. Almost immediately after entering the *Tunnel* he was bowled over by two SAMs. SAM's were special international police, Secular Army Marshals, who had begun to become a welcomed presence in open source virtual reality, and sometimes in physical reality as well, depending on your community's security needs.

Han fell but rolled up quickly, metal fighting bar in hand. "Ĉesu ke ŝtelisto!" one of the new world cops shouted, before disappearing into the dark end of the corridor. A bright light flashed from the black void and temporarily had Han seeing orange. He decided to walk the other way, quickly.

Getting robbed virtually sounded terrifying. Because every VIP visitor was always a physical door away from blipping out thieves had to hold their victims down. Apparently the only thing comparable to getting virtually smothered was to get physically water boarded. Unable to move, virtual criminals would seal the mouths of their prey until all coin was given up and transferred over.

As Han's vision came into focus he saw that the four branches of the U.S. military had set up shop recently in the new gaming world. The VIP would one day be full of potential recruits, many with virtual reality programming skills; it made sense Han guessed. Religious groups, travel agents, college fraternities, doctors, body workers, tutors, propagandists, were all accessible through The Tunnel. VIP wasn't illegal, and some compared it to a designer drug that's just hit the street; everybody who knew about it wanted a piece of it. Several of the rooms, like the Ultimate Underground, even had their own underground TV channels. If it were to become regulated any time soon, many fans wanted to enjoy it while it lasted, or just figure out how to get on the ground floor of the consumer platform of the future.

Army, Navy, Air force, Marines, International Secular Army, Island Vacations, Space Travel, Undersea Adventure, African Safari, Surfer Central, High Peak Snowboarding, Fortune Tellers, Chess, Japanese Baseball, American Football, a dozen types of massage parlors, *Ultimate Underground, Donnybrook, Old School Arcade,* and a myriad of dating services, were all neon signs that Han passed within his first five minutes inside. Almost everything that interested him required payment, but Han was hoping to explore the fun stuff when he had company to share it with.

"Spare coin?" someone wearing a rag strewn avatar asked him.

"Sorry," Han replied, checking behind him after that periodically to see if he were being followed.

"Left! Left! Left! Right! Left!" yelled a line of Marines as they jogged by in synch.

"C'mon in…" invited a woman who appeared under a XXX sign, "we don't bite."

Han kept walking, and sped up even faster when he got to the doors that had no signs at all above them. How many rooms were there he wondered, and how many average people are trying to program the next best virtual experience? The room he finally decided on to enter, for the fee of a sixteenth of a coin, had a sign over its door that read *Petting Zoo*.

Han retrieved his coin card from his armor and slid it at the zoo's entrance. As he walked in the digital scene settled into his view. He realized that he had picked a popular site. Families were circling, reaching out to touch, and sometimes leaped back in fear of seemingly wild animals.

———

Neimann Marcuss, Saks off Fifth, Burberry, were all names he had heard Lenora mention as stores she'd go to when she visited him on the East Coast. Maybe though, he could beat her to the punch and send her something special? As he browsed through endless rows of blouses and dresses he began to feel utterly helpless. A sales person began to hover. "Let me know if I can be of any assistance," she said. Aeson ignored her, not wanting to look into the cold eyes of another android. "Or not…" she finished, thinking that Aeson was just another rude person coming to Jersey to shop in order to beat the sales tax.

Instead of calling on the services of a potential robot employee Aeson left the clothing store and fell into a sea of distracted people.

Teenagers were everywhere, holding hands, pushing each other, picking food out of their braces. Strollers looked as if they were being steered by the babies inside them while the mothers careened their necks wildly in search of sales. A man on a slow moving motorcycle rode around as if he were the coolest person in the entire state.

Females, younger, older, and the same age ogled Aeson Cadmus as if he were a piece of meat and they were extremely hungry carnivores. One girl kept looking at her phone, then up at Aeson, then back at her phone. "Aeson Cadmus!" she screamed, "You kicked Guido's ass last night!" Aeson's brain wouldn't accept the reality of actual fans from his first virtual fight screaming at him in a mall; until she started after him in a fast walk, then a jog, and finally a full sprint. She had a pack of her friends in tow. Aeson heard one yell "Hot Cage Fighter!" just before he ducked into a jewelry store.

"How may we help dear?" an elegant older woman who donned massive pearl earrings asked him.

The fighter's eyes scanned shelves of glittering necklaces, bracelets, and rings.

"Can you show me where the engagement rings are?"

———

Han walked by a group he thought may have been from Greece. One of the kids reached out to touch him saying, "Geeta, eena mai-moo!" Han's hand gently came up to parry the curious fingers. The child's father snatched his daughter up, afraid that Han, an armored simian in a zoo, might be dangerous.

Han ignored the Greeks' shock, for his own weighed heavier on his heart. Another child, from China, was screaming "Shizi!" while reaching out to pull the mane of a great and kingly cat. The lion looked bewildered as the child pulled, oblivious, in its own VIP room somewhere, of why its own mane was moving.

When Han walked by he heard one of the Chinese parents whisper, "Sun Wukong..."

The entrance booth had a lengthy explanation about the safety of each display, but when Han saw a virtually free boa constrictor of some fifteen feet in length, he shook his head at the room's owner's ignorance. Perhaps the lion was in its own VIP room somewhere, sedated most likely, and covered in the 3-D printed giant cat version of a nano-suit minus the goggles. The boa constrictor however looked like it was moving quickly, a sign that it was not sedated, or fed. Han had learned from watching Aeson's fight that a strong grip in the VIP world can do a lot of damage.

Han followed a sign that read *Great Apes* in several different languages. When he arrived there was barely room to get by. Han nudged his way through to find visitors tickling, shoving, and even hitting several confused and obviously inebriated chimpanzees. Han's hands clenched into fists and he experienced an anger that not even Aeson's pre-workout meditation could summon. When he saw two fraternity boys forcing a pledge to hold hands with a young female bonobo, his emotion could not be contained.

"No!" Han yelled as he leapt into the air, spinning his metal bat as if it were a helicopter's blades. The frat boys fell to the ground and shielded their faces under their arms. "What's going on!" one yelled.

"This is crazy!" screamed the pledge in terror, "I'm logging off!"

"No you're not! Delta E used all of the alumni donations on this VIP shit. You leave now and you're not in!" commanded the leader of the new form of hazing.

Han took the zealous leader's legs out from under him with his staff. As soon as he tried to stand up the Chinese god of trickery placed a red booted foot on top of his chest.

"Listen to me! All of you!" Han cried. "It's obvious you are from all over this planet..."

Visitors stared in awe of Han's avatar. Han heard an employee say, "Ask if we can borrow a security guard from the Porn Palace. Go."

Security, Han thought, bring him on. In a lawless world, those who establish themselves are the law.

"You've come from many different countries, and follow your own customs. Well I'm telling you right now, that anything you've ever learned about animals not being equal to people is wrong! Look at yourselves! Mocking these innocent creatures!"

An automatic recording played on a timer, "We have made sure that all our animals are having the best possible experience. Watch as the bonobo gets "friendly."

"You are always at war or on the brink of it! The bonobo, and all the ape people, live in harmony with our dwindling environment, you just..."

Before Han could finish venting what had probably been bottled up for years a terrified scream pulled at everyone's attention.

"Help! The snake has our baby!"

One of the frat boys disappeared, along with several foreign tourists, most followed Han towards the pleading father.

The constrictor had completely wrapped up a seven year old boy with its long, muscular body. The boy could be heard giggling, probably feeling initially something akin to a tickle. Han knew that it was only a matter of time for the snake to do what it was designed to do to prey.

"Get your kid out of the VIP!" Han ordered. "Open the door and get off line!"

"I can't!" shouted the father. He was fruitlessly pulling on the snake's thick mass, "I'm on a work trip, my wife just ran out to the store, it's right near our house but my son's home alone."

"Alone? Are you kidding me!" Han scolded.

"We have a smart-house, there's never been any problems. Please! Whoever, or whatever you are, please save my son."

Han pushed the begging dad off the boa and mounted the hungry beast. Han located its head and slid his fighting staff into its mouth and beneath its teeth. The amount of strength it takes to separate a boa from its prey in the real world is impossible to summon for one person. In the virtual world, even more force is required to act on the nano-suit. Han gripped his staff with both hands, used a rowing motion, and leaned back with all his might. The child had stopped giggling and Han feared that he was already unconscious.

Every patron of the Zoo room seemed to be cheering Han on. A primal and powerful scream fired out of Han's throat, "Yeeeee!" and the different ape communities began screaming in support. "Yeeee! Yeeee! Yeeee!" The jaws began to open and Han wrapped both his legs around its neck. He pulled up and squeezed in at the same time, creating just enough space for the small child to crawl to safety.

"Thank you! Thank you!" cried the tearful father as he knelt down and took his virtual son in his hands. "What... what is your name?"

Han scanned the crowd as the python curled itself up, confused probably as to how its victim escaped. Han saw people who looked like they had just been shaken awake. He hated them for supporting such a place, but pitied them for being so sheepish. "You should not support this room, or any rooms like it. Virtual reality is not an excuse to forget your values. All creatures, all life, deserves respect. And you tell your friends and family what I've said."

"Please, sir... who are you, who do I thank?"

Han felt, and not for the first time in his life, separate from all species, only difference now was, he was fine with it.

"Who am I? I'm Monkey King."

———

The jewelry store did not take, or even know what VIPcoin was. Their bank, though, instantly converted Aeson's money upon his purchase. The ring cost most of his winnings, but, after he signed the contract, there'd be plenty more where it came from. He couldn't wait to tell her, certainly not until she visited. He had thrown caution out to buy the thing, so now he was going to crush caution by calling Lenora, and ask her to marry him.

"Babe, Lenora, you got a minute?"

"Sure."

She didn't sound her usual self, but Aeson wasn't his usual self either, and his awareness was clouded by the excitement of his upcoming bold move.

"I have a surprise."

"Oh, it's not a surprise Aeson. I know you're fighting in the Ultimate Underground. I use the internet!"

"Well, it's not, well, that's part of it, but..."

"I saw you kiss that woman, Aeson. Big virtual superstar now! What's next Aeson! Was that your surprise, or were you calling to break up with me. Didn't you take that job, move all the way across the country, to help a special needs kid? I got to go. Hope you're having fun."

Aeson closed his eyes in utter disbelief and felt the pangs of depression quickly convert into anger, and then action.

"You have a return policy right?"

An hour later Aeson answered a call through his new helmet's phone. "No thanks Sal. I'll find my way back." The new motorcycle felt like a metal horse, no, a winged metal horse, and Aeson was eager to fly to places he had never been to.

Chapter 9
THE TUNNEL

"You can't tell our customers to not come back here!" a worker from the virtual *Petting Zoo* commanded Han.

Han looked around, and saw one by one visitors walking out.

"Is this the guy who's giving your business a problem?" a hulking figure stepped in to question.

"Yeah! This is him. A rebel rouser. Please, get him the hell outta here," spoke the zoo's representative. "We also own two massage parlors. Free entry for you and yours if you take care of this."

The bouncer, dressed in all black, was bald, unnaturally muscular from synthetic growth hormones, and itching to get physical. He looked at Han from beneath his extended Neanderthal-like brow with only animosity in his eyes; "Let's go freak."

As he approached Han a mild mannered visitor using a generic avatar tried to intervene, "This freak just saved a kid's life you gerks!"

"This room sucks!" someone else shouted, "I'd like my coin back!"

"I'd rather take my kids elsewhere!"

"Wo men qu ba!"

"Pame!"

"Yah-lah!"

The exodus only enraged the bouncer further. He grabbed Han by his armored chest plate and lifted him off the ground.

"Is everyone seeing this!" Han shouted.

The crowd shouted back in at least five different languages to put Han down.

The virtual *Petting Zoo* worker responded with, "We're trying to run a business here!"

The kid Han saved from the boa's grasp murmured with difficulty but with great concern, "Weave, Monkey King a-wone!"

"So, there are witnesses now," Han reminded as he looked directly into his assailant's eyes.

"I guess so. Freak!"

With that Han felt a confidence he had never experienced before. The energy of the fight meditation that Aeson had taught him flashed before his mind's eye like the brightest lightning. Monkey King lifted his knees and pushed his heels into the man's chest, sending the bouncer flying backwards and himself gracefully into the virtual air while coiled up in a backflip.

The animals, although they were supposed to be blind to the room's experience, began to fill the zoo with growls, howls, screams, and cries. The bald security guard was rising up to take another shot at Han as a paw, bigger than his head, pressed down upon his shoulder and pinned him. The lion's toothless virtual mouth covered the entirety of the bouncer's face. The security guard reached his hand out blindly and felt for the door of his own VIP room. As he pulled it open he blipped out of the *Petting Zoo* and out of the VIP world. The zoo worker was left to face Monkey King alone. At least a dozen visitors wanted to throw him to the lion. Han had something else in mind. Before he could make an emergency exit Han had him on his shoulder and was carrying him to have a face to face meeting with a Silver Back gorilla.

———

Aeson glided through the packed parking lot, onto the busy highway, then towards Newark. Lenora's words stung him like his first busted lip. It was a shock and a call to action. Forget malls, seeing sights, visiting New York City. The kid was special, and he hired a coach to help him.

Where had that lady dropped me off? Aeson wondered. I was so cloudy from the anger management medication I'm having a tough time remembering. He slowed the new bike down every time he thought he was closer, only to attract looks from locals, some curious, some seemingly hostile.

"Nice ride man."

"Don't come here to buy your drugs punk!"

"You make a wrong turn on that fancy bike!"

"Wanna date?"

It was nearing five o'clock when he glided down the alley and in front of the door that read *Jeet Kune Do*.

"Oh I remember you, Aeson Cadmus. From the looks of that new bike seems like things, for you, are working out."

Aeson was flooded with memories and feelings of gratitude.

"Nothing would have worked out if you hadn't given me a ride to my job interview Sifu. I just want to thank you for helping me when I was in trouble," Aeson said, and began to reach for his phone to offer a VIPcoin transfer.

"Put that away Aeson. The way of the warrior bro. You needed help, and I had the means. You want to thank me then go get changed in the locker room. Class starts in five minutes, and some of my students would love to mix it up with someone new."

Their hands moved and whirled with intensity and precision. The sifu used Aeson to demonstrate techniques that worked against trained fighters. Aeson was heartily impressed, but not surprised. His father had grilled into him the importance of being open to all styles, and this kind and strong Newark master seemed to embody the perfect martial artist. "Hand here. Knee bent. Soften your grasp. Stay fluid, like a snake, before it strikes!" Aeson could hear the sifu guiding the dozen students who were made up of half a dozen different ethnicities, some who did not speak English well, towards higher learning, both in self-defense, and in character development.

After class Sifu and Aeson had tea. "You told us tonight in class to be formless. Do you mean the best fighters shouldn't have a style?"

"I never said that Aeson. You've seen Bruce Lee's movies right?"

"My dad used to show them to me, yeah."

"Well, maybe you don't remember how Sifu Lee described formless. He said be like water. Water doesn't fight the tea pot, it becomes the teapot."

"But, what is the tea pot? Some sort of metaphor?"

"It's your true self Aeson. The part of you that is perfect."

"Philosophical," said the fighter, deciding then that he had learned enough for one day. "You're a great fighter and a great teacher Sifu. I hope I can become half the martial artist you are someday."

"I simply encourage everyone to research their own experiences Aeson. Different techniques, and even fighting itself, is just a vehicle to do that."

Aeson realized he had to ask one more question, "What if the vehicle I give to my student doesn't work for him, or even for his body type?"

"Oh, well, there are many paths, just like there are many styles of Kung-Fu. In this day and age we have the benefit of information. Find a style that works for him."

As the sweat cooled on Aeson's face his mind became warm with memory. The homeless couple, the ones who nearly got him killed but also saved the day popped into his consciousness. "The couple who introduced me to you...?"

"Jacob and LuLu?"

"Yes! The woman had a style of fighting that would be perfect for the kid I'm working with."

"Oh LuLu, poor thing. Her and Jacob were instructors here once. LuLu practiced her Kung Fu incessantly and taught it with proficiency."

"What happened to them? Drugs?"

"Drugs sure happened, but that came after their son was killed, right over on Muhammad Ali Ave. Gunned down for who knows what."

"That's really horrible Sifu. So now she's on the streets with a head full of knowledge..."

"And a heart full of grief," finished the regal looking teacher of Jeet-Kune-Do.

"What is her style of fighting Sifu?"

"A very powerful system, primal yet elegant, unpredictable yet precise."

"Monkey Kung-Fu right?"

"Yes but there are many Monkey systems: *Lost Monkey, Wooden Monkey, Stone Monkey, Drunken Monkey,* and others that I've never even seen before. She's the only person I've ever known to master all of them."

———

Han headed straight to *Valhalla.* Wait till Katie hears about this Petting Zoo, she'll be furious! Odin too. I hope those tourists don't ever go back there. And that bouncer's going to think twice before getting in the way of someone voicing their honest opinion.

As Han walked the *Tunnel,* no longer as astonished at the sight of new neon room signs, he began to wonder if he had done the right thing. Of course it was right he decided! Those… animals don't deserve to be treated like that. Life inside a box, no contact with others, is no life at all. But did I have to kick him so hard? And… I don't feel good about making the other guy cry, but, he deserved it, and the gorilla was just playing.

The Old School Arcade room sang with the tweets, buzzers, and dings of *Pac Man, Galaga,* and *Donkey Kong* as Han walked by. Next time, Han thought, and with Aeson, Katya, Odin, and even Al and Sal. My uncles would probably love that room. Might remind them of the old days or something, when gaming first started.

Han walked and walked through the *Tunnel* until he began to lose track of time. He searched dark alleys, was solicited by avatar designers, virtual wine merchants, and supposed employers who promised wealth and status.

"Trade in that costume for a soldier's uniform!" a voice announced from a recruiter's office.

"God is here my son, come to our room of worship," another softly requested.

Han kept walking, not caring if he got lost because his VIP door was just feet away from his real body. Thirst began to beckon, but his new sense of himself as someone who had strength, even power, and the wherewithal to use it justly, continued to energize him.

A hooded figure who modeled his outfit off of a seventeenth century assassin's appeared out of nowhere, as most *Tunnel* walkers did, and was charging, more than briskly, straight at Han. He almost jumped out of the way to avoid the freight train pace of this shady character, but at the last second Monkey King stood his ground. If he wants me to move he should at least say excuse me. The faceless speed walker stretched out both his arms, he was going to try and push Han out of the way and keep going. Han breathed in, rolled his shoulders back, and gave the man his target. Upon impact, it was the hooded figure who fell.

Monkey King stood over the cloaked man, then took a step back when he made a quick movement. The shadowy figure extended his hands again, as if to defend himself against Han. Han gripped both his wrists, and picked him up in one swift movement. Standing him back up on his feet accidently caused his hood to fall away.

"Please, I have no coin, just passing through."

The man Han picked up was actually a boy who wore virtual clothing over his true form. "What? You think I'm going to rob you?"

"I don't know, maybe, but, there's something else, behind you, it's coming!" The boy took off again running with his arms extended stiff as metal.

"Relax! I don't rob people!" Han pleaded, saddened by the kid's outright fear, and feeling the same sense of justice he felt in the zoo rear up again. As the hooded kid disappeared Han thought about all the apparent crime happening in the Tunnel. He wondered if the kid's warning was just a ploy. He turned around to continue his explorations and saw what the frightened boy was talking about.

"You the Monkey King?" asked a floating statue, white like marble, with nothing actually moving save for the hands and eyes. At first glance Han too felt afraid, for one of the hands held a large hammer, the other, a ball of fire. "Well? Can't you speak? Don't tell me you're scared," the floating, ghostly statue of a bearded god questioned.

"Nope, I just never met a talking statue before," Han replied.

"Well I've never met a real simian human hybrid before," said the spectral form back. Its mouth hadn't moved, only its fingers, which tickled the air as if typing. The content of its speech shocked Han even more than its ghostly holographic appearance.

"Glad you like my avatar," Han responded, not wanting to believe that the figure before him could actually know his secret.

"I write VIP code, and I can tell the difference between avatar and nano-outline from a mile away."

Han froze, then felt himself stumble.

"Relax man. I'm Hephaestos," the all-knowing specter announced as he stretched out the fingers of his right hand in a gesture of greeting, his face frozen in a permanent glare, the eyes held in a forger's squint. "Your secret's safe with me if that's what you want. I heard about what you did in that pathetic zoo, and I want to speak with you, that's all. I can use a real ass kicker who's got an actual conscience. Somebody to watch my back, and help me clean this place up. Now shake my hand, I can't do all the talking with my left."

Han stretched his arm out and took hold of the soft fragile appendage.

"C'mon Monkey King! Squeeze it! I can barely feel a handshake in the real world. You're not gonna hurt me," Hephaestos demanded with his right hand gripped within Han's and his left fingers moving rapidly.

Han increased his pressure while taking in more detail. Hephaestos glowed with a white achromatic aura and his virtual eyes moved with an eagerness to live. Han wanted to trust this new VIP person, but felt like the *Tunnel* was too impersonal.

"Ever been to *Valhalla* ?" Han asked.

"Hah! Of course I've been there. I designed that room for a guy from Alpine."

———

LuLu was right where the Sifu said she would be, Muhammad Ali Ave. She paced the block and talked to herself in Mandarin. Winter was coming to an end, but she remained dressed for the Antarctic. If she slowed down she might appear to be a pile of old clothes rolling down the sidewalk on its own accord. She wasn't walking slowly though; her feet were trying to match the pace in her head. "Wèishéme!" she screamed whenever anyone walked by her.

Aeson parked his motorcycle just up the block from her, and walked towards her carefully. She stopped before he could get too close, scrunched her face as if she had just bitten into a lemon, and shouted her mantra of the day, "Wèishéme!"

Aeson did not know how to respond, so he did what he saw everyone do in the Jeet-Kune-Do school. It was what he called the Kung-Fu salute. Aeson made a fist with his right hand and placed his left open palm on top of it. Lulu reflexively returned the gesture. When Aeson began to introduce himself however, Lulu became visibly upset.

"I'm sorry," Aeson told her, "I didn't mean to bother you."

"Lu! Don't hurt that man now," came Jacob's warning from behind a garbage can. See his bike, maybe he's got some cash!"

"What chou want crackah!" Lulu screamed.

"To learn Kung-Fu. I have a student actually, I think Monkey is the best style for him," Aeson explained.

Lulu peered more and more closely into Aeson's face, "You here two weeks ago, you have Synth for me?"

"Synth?" the fighter wondered before realizing, "Oh, the Synthoazapine. My anger management meds. I stopped taking them actually, feel much better..."

"Ahhhhh! Go home cracka, you know nothing of my Kung-Fu. Too good to give me your Synth, no deserve my style."

Aeson started to plead again and was about to offer money when Lulu's demeanor changed to combative. Her head bobbed fluidly from side to say as did her shoulders. Her wrists bent and her hands formed fists. Her stance lowered and the fighter could have sworn he heard her skeleton popping into readiness.

"Look... Miss Lulu, I..."

"You better get on your bike and go back to wherever it is you came from while you still can," said Jacob, now standing to his full height.

"I didn't mean to..." Aeson tried to explain.

"If you don't act soon," Jacob said, pointing up the road to where Aeson had parked, "you might be stuck here."

Aeson looked at Lulu who was shaking with an energy that made the fighter take a step back, then at Jacob who was still pointing, and then back at his new motorcycle, which he now realized was being stolen.

"I wouldn't do that if I was you!" Aeson warned a man dressed in over-sized camouflage who had already mounted Aeson's new steed and was attempting to do something to its console with a screwdriver.

"Mine now sucka!" the bike thief yelled with a smile while attempting to hot wire the high tech bike.

"I warned you!" Aeson reiterated as he walked towards the scene.

Suddenly the bike began to raise its front wheel, place it down, just before raising the back tire up and balancing on the front.

"What the!" shouted the bike thief. The vehicle began to increase the height and speed of its mechanical bucking motion.

"I told you!" Aeson reiterated, getting increasingly worried about his motorcycle's security system's ability to incapacitate its hijacker; not to mention all the attention it might attract.

"I am being stolen! Police! Someone is attempting to unlawfully acquire me! I am being stolen!" the machine alarmed.

Aeson looked back and Lulu and Jacob were gone. He knew that if he got to his bike before its initial warning he might have time to stop it.

The thief was now screaming, his screwdriver tossed uncontrollably and his hands desperately tried to cling to the handlebars. "Ahhhhh!" he screamed as the padding around the bike's grips heated up to unbearable temperatures, "Ahhhh!"

Its bucking motion increased every three seconds, and the man could only tighten his knees and scream. A group of kids saw what was happening from their apartment's window and began to shout down laughter. A car slowed to check out the scene and began recording it with a phone. Aeson sprinted into position and put up his hands as if it were one of Lenora's horses gone out of control. He tried to remember what he was told about disengaging the system but could only shout, "It's me Aeson Cadmus, your owner, you're not being stolen!" By the third time, as if the bike had to hear it enough to believe it, the machine came to a halt. The second it came to a standstill Aeson took hold of the would-be thief and threw his already dizzy form to the ground. The laughter and cat calls grew louder. Aeson searched the perimeter for Lulu but thought it best to try again later. The fighter jumped on his new transportation and quickly had the bike moving.

As he rode down the avenue however, he spotted a nest of three trees, one of which was marked by a Chinese Symbol. A tarp was tied to create a small shelter. Aeson knew where he was going to look when he returned, and next time, he'd bring exactly what Lulu wanted.

———

Katie Carouche drove up and down Palisades Interstate parkway scouting out a good hiding spot for the Chinook camper she had borrowed from Mr. Senga. Nearing sun down, she turned the ignition off and stretched out. The Palisades were cliffs that overlooked the Hudson River, and lay in between New York City and the high end New Jersey town where the Zucharinos had built their home.

The vehicle she drove had all the amenities of a small apartment. She knew that there were secret, hidden things as well; things that Mr. Senga had trained her husband to use. As she climbed in the back Katie was surprised at just how roomy it was. She noticed that the floor, as well as the ceiling, and the walls, once she moved things out of the way, were padded, and that nothing ordinary was actually as it seemed. There was an adjustable solar panel on the roof, as well as a satellite dish, despite the Chinook's older appearance. When she pulled out what was supposed to be a kitchen cutting board, a computer screen opened. She sipped from a can of cold green tea she found and logged on.

Hey Han. Katya here. You around?

Three heavy knocks rapped on the back door of the still cooling camper. Katie pressed send, and took a deep breath before addressing whoever was visiting her secret location.

————

Despite having promised Han his afternoon lesson, Aeson slowed his motorcycle down. He felt compelled to take things in, and to learn more about this new world he was residing in. Newark had rough streets, like where Lulu and Jacob lived, and it also had office buildings and more elite neighborhoods. It seemed like one block could be a recovering war zone, while another glistened with modern smart structures, impressive art, and new world security.

Secular Army Marshalls patrolled with robot dogs in tow, keeping the citizenry safe and unafraid. Aeson had never seen these high tech guardians before, only in film, and wondered what kind of presence they held across the river in New York City. NYC, the borough of Queens to be exact, was only two years out of from its last terrorist attack.

Aeson had watched Queens burn and explode on TV in a local mountain bar. When terrorism hit the Big Apple that time he'd thought surely he'd never travel east. Life goes on, and he figured that surrendering to fear was still surrendering. And surrender just wasn't in his blood.

————

The tree felt like the best place to go after being in the VIP for so long. The cold air, and as the sun went down, the glistening view of the giant cable bridge called George Washington, was what Han needed to look at to re-engage with the non-virtual world. He thought about Hephaestos, his new friend, and how they were less than an hour from each other in the real world. He brought his phone but wanted to be more alert before he returned Katya's message. He closed his eyes and tried to separate the sounds of swishing cars from those made by nature. When he opened his eyes a chickadee was on his knee. Han and the little bird met stares and seemed to be admiring each other. Han smiled and the bird remained. He moved his hand, and still the tiny creature did not budge. He reached slowly towards the black capped dinosaur, and instead of flying away, it hopped onto his finger.

"Han! You up there? It's Aeson!"

"Coach!" Han eagerly replied. The bird disappeared as Han lowered the rope ladder.

"I'm sorry we missed training man," apologized Aeson, "but wait till I tell you about my day."

Han listened in vicarious enjoyment, but felt a longing to leave his own roost. He laughed so hard about the new motorcycle's security system that he nearly bounced out of the tree. As the two climbed down to head into the house Han congratulated his coach on his Ultimate Underground contract.

"Thanks Han. I know I'll be able do well, and it won't take away at all from your experience, I promise."

"Speaking of my experience..."

"Uh huh..."

"I've never been on a motorcycle before, and we have an extra helmet. Do you think ...?"

"Let's do it," Aeson replied after only a small pause. "We'll just time it when everyone else is out, then take her for a spin."

"Awesome!"

Chapter 10
OUTSIDE

The bed was soft, and perfectly warm from the heat of both their bodies. She had never felt so strongly for anyone.

He was incredibly handsome, sensitive in his own way, and so very dangerous. Now she was married to him. She watched as the clean white sheet moved with his slow breathing. Even in a deep sleep he seemed ready for anything.

His work took him to so many interesting places, and the money he made on a single job was more than she could earn in a whole year in the U.S. Army. She had loved the military; the discipline, the training, the weapons, were all fun for her. But when he offered her something new, a whole lifestyle change, she was ecstatic.

Majstro, as he was referred to, was once in the service, but she knew better than to ask him about it. When her term was up, he did just what he said he would do. They tied the knot in a special ceremony, most everything was in Japanese, which she didn't really understand, but that didn't matter. She was his, and he was hers.

Maj was waking, slowly stretching from beneath the comfortable fabric. The two had woken up together in so many foreign lands. They met in Iran after all, where she helped train female bodyguards who protected U.S. allies. He was there for work as well, it was a private contractor job, that's all she knew at the time.

"Honey... are you awake?" she whispered, not wanting to intrude on his dreams.

"Yes, yes dear, I'm awake," he responded, sounding more alert than Katie had originally thought.

"Well, what do you want to do today?" she gently asked.

"What do I want to do?"

"Yes sweetie, I want to know what you want. I don't even know what hotel, or even city we're in – Tokyo, New York, Moscow? But whatever you desire, I'm sure it will be fun."

"Fun..." whispered from beneath the bedding, then all went silent, and his movement, even his steady breathing, seemed to stop.

"Honey, Majstro, wake up. Maj, Maj..." she said as she shook him with both her hands, "Maj!"

His torso shot straight up, as if spring loaded, sending the white sheet off of him. His skin was completely green and appeared covered with fungus and moss. His body had the form of well-developed human muscle, but it was not flesh, it was green, vegetable, cellulose. His eyes were buried within a tangle of roots that intertwined around his whole face, and Katie thought that they looked like small bright yellow sunflowers. His shoulders were as wide and seemingly as strong as an oak tree. His hands were big but dexterous and appeared to have small twigs protruding from the tips.

"I want to live! I want to get out of this bed and live!" he yelled in an unearthly tone that had Katie gasping in fear. His fibrous hands were around her neck and they began to squeeze. The small yellow daisies he had for pupils began to spin as he looked into her eyes, now whispering a throat scratching command; "Help me Katie, help me, or I will never return from this."

"I think you're having a nightmare miss, I heard you screaming. Is everything OK?"

Katie woke in the dark hull of the Chinook camper. She was sleeping alone, sweat soaked from a nightmare. It was cold outside of her sleeping bag, and that nosy backpacker was at the door again.

———

Han still in his pajamas slid his feet as he walked across the white stone tiles.

"Get this guy an expresso Al," said Uncle Sal jokingly, reaching out for a high five from his nephew only to be left hanging. Han slid towards Aeson and they fist bumped without looking at each other. "Oh, I see how it is," Sal complained, and told Al, "Kids, unbelievable right?"

Al responded, still in his black silk pajamas, "Right. Kids. Where's the respect?"

"Let's start the day right young man," said Stella to Han, as she handed her son and Aeson each a health shake.

"There kiwis in mine mom?" asked Han, his eyes only half opened.

"Yes, yours is an energy drink, and I know you love your kiwis baby," assured Stella. "And Aeson, yours has peanut butter in it. I figured you could use the protein.

"Thanks Stella," Aeson said before taking a swig and coming up with a mustache of foam over his upper lip.

"Of course Aeson, and just so you know I put the same amount of the Babazuke's Rage-No-More supplement in as last time. You should never need those pills again."

"Oh no," said Sal, "the Fighter is in training, and we don't need no passive performances. Don't drink that Aeson."

Han and Aeson looked at Uncle Sal with wide eyes, suddenly both extremely awake, as if to say, "Shutup! Remember Aeson's Ultimate Underground work is still secret!"

"I know what's going on you two, don't worry, Grandpa told me, and I support it. Sounds much better than actually getting your brains beat in in real life. And you Sal, maybe you should drink a shake instead of all those cocktails."

Aeson sighed in relief, then pushed the rest of the shake aside. "Maybe I'll just finish it later."

"Suit yourself hon, I'll put it in a container for you." Stella's hair was pulled back in a ponytail and she was wearing a tank top. Aeson couldn't help but notice her chiseled arms, rock hard shoulders, and sinewy neck.

She lived a healthy lifestyle, that was for sure. Aeson looked at Han, then back at Stella, and had to wonder what Han's father looked like. "You guys gonna train hard today?" Stella asked her son and his personal coach.

They both answered at the same time, nearly incriminating themselves with feigned innocence, "Yes!"

"Well, I want to see your stuff later, show me some of these moves Aeson's teaching you. And don't forget your humanities project. You can't have an extension on it forever."

"I know mom, I'm on it."

"Love you guys," Stella told them, sending a warm feeling through Aeson's heart. Over the last few weeks this teaching gig has become way more than a job, the fighter thought, the Zucharinos are like my family.

"The rematch is coming up guy, stay limber, and drink a lot of water," said Sal, as he too prepared for a day out somewhere with Al.

Aeson felt prepared for his next UU fight. He wasn't worried. He had kept up on his training and had been spending more and more time in the VIP. Aeson's concern was Han, and as the kid's coach, he had to help him. They had been hatching their plan ever since Aeson bought his own ride, but had to wait for the day when everyone would be out.

Han looked out the window as the cars pulled away, "OK, I'll get the extra helmet."

"Keep your voice down dude, your grandpa is napping," reminded Aeson.

"Sorry," replied Han in a whisper.

"Did you take care of our cover?" asked Aeson.

"I set up the audio from our last workout in the gym to trigger every time someone opens the door."

"Awesome Han, you're a regular James Bond," Aeson complimented his protégé for his technical savvy as he pocketed the pills he promised LuLu. He also packed a satchel full of Babazuke health snacks and double checked the Sifu's text message about what time he could use the backroom of the Dojang.

They rolled the motorcycle out of the side door of the large garage. Han mounted the seat behind his coach and looked back at the house and at the moving security cameras that followed their exit.

———

"You OK? I just want to make sure," asked the hiker again.

Katie's jaw clenched down and her fists shook with tension. She wanted to blast the back door open with a side kick then beat the hell out of this annoying, and very smelly hiker.

"I'm fine! Please go away now," ordered the increasingly livid Katie Carouche.

"Oh I'm sorry. I just heard you scream and wanted to make sure you're OK, that's all."

"Alright. Enough. I get it, you're a do gooder and I was in distress. I hope you feel better about your life. Now…"

"Hey, that's not really that nice. Ya know this is the problem with the world today. People just aren't gracious…"

Katie was sitting up now, rubbing the nightmare from her eyes and hair, pulling on a sweatshirt, and preparing to unleash terror upon this annoying individual. She turned the handle of the backdoor and decided not to kick it open. She thought it better to walk out so he had no warning to run or even to defend himself. She would daintily hop out, manage a smile, and then begin the beat-down that would send this loser packing.

She could see her breath as the door opened, the morning sun beamed behind the man's scraggly head, making his damp red beard glisten. Other than the early morning chill the remnants of Winter were gone and the various species of trees were budding. Something on the man's chest glistened brighter than his dew wet facial hair. A golden badge that read *US Park Ranger Office of the Interior* made her second guess her decision to greet her visitor with an elbow to the face. Instead of breaking his jaw she gritted her teeth, called upon the little training that Mr. Senga had given her in self-control, and said "Good morning sir."

———

"So this guy you met in the VIP is cool?" asked Aeson as they turned onto the Palisades Parkway.

"Yeah, really cool, his name's Steven, but his virtual tag is Hephaestus."

"That is cool."

Han was so excited about all the new changes in his life he wanted to scream as his bonobo genetics recommended, but he held back. He played it as calm as he could. He could hardly believe that Aeson was going to take him to a real martial arts school and he was still in a state of shock over the confidence him and his new friend had already put in each other.

"He actually lives in Newark, near to where we're going," Han told his coach hesitantly.

"Really?" asked Aeson, and before his young student could ask him his coach offered, "Well should we pay him a visit before training."

"Yeeeee!" came out of Han's happiest self and nearly deafened the driver.

"I guess that's a yes."

Han called Steven as they drove. If he answers, Han thought, his computer will have to convert Steven's text to speech.

"Hello Han," answered Steven, "are you mobile right now?"

"Yeah man, I'm outta the house, and am going to be in your neck of the woods!"

"You saying you're stopping by here?"

"Is that cool?" asked Han, not used to arranging meetings in the real world.

"Sure! You'll probably have to meet my aunt though."

Han paused, as they passed an auto-piloted car with a sleeping driver in it.

"Be there in a half hour!"

———

"I really didn't mean to bother you it's just that…"

"I know, you heard me scream, and I appreciate that. Look, I'm a veteran," said Katie, appealing to the Ranger's patriotism, "and, let's just say, I'm traveling by myself to try to get some things straight."

"PTSD, I get it. Well, the wilderness is healing, that's why I do what I do."

"Are you patrolling the Palisades?"

"Believe it or not I'm on a special duty. I'm hiking from Maine and going all the way across the country, recording stories and experiences that we could use to inspire improvement of the trail systems. You are actually a perfect example of why we need to keep the trails alive."

"Well, great," Katie responded, letting her anger turn into calculated decision making, "thanks for your support."

"Hey, coffee's on. Want a cup?"

"Sure, yeah, coffee sounds good, then I'm going to do my journaling. The docs at the V.A. say it's important." She looked around and saw his tent, camp stove, and percolating brew. Katie was disappointed in herself that she didn't hear him come in at night. She made a promise to be more aware but resolved herself to entertain this Park Ranger, and make it look realistic until he finished his stay.

———

Aeson and Han were slowed down by traffic, but were enjoying their first conversation had outside of the house.

"Steven's going to teach me how to VIP code, and I'm going to make sure he feels safe in the Tunnel."

"Sounds like a win win situation. Are you going to teach him the basics of self-defense?"

"He was in an accident three years ago, well... not really an accident. The Queen's Jihad is what a lot of people still call it. It was a religious war between Christians, Muslims, Jews, even Hindus and Buddhists got involved."

"Oh I heard about it. It's the main reason why Lenora didn't want me to take the job with you guys. She thinks the East Coast is crazy and more stuff like that can happen anytime."

"I've never been to New York City, but from what I've seen online and heard from Al and Sal things are pretty safe, the Secular Army makes sure of that."

"That's good, I guess," said Aeson, remembering all of his father's warnings about the importance of self-sufficiency, especially when it came to personal security. "Maybe you and I can visit New York, you know Central Park, Times Square, all that tourist stuff."

"Sounds great!" Han shouted, making Aeson wince and smile at the same time.

The bike took the Newark exit and slowed down while Aeson followed the directions on his helmet screen.

"So, how bad did your friend get hurt?"

"Real bad, his building was bombed, from what I can tell, he's almost totally paralyzed. His whole family got killed so he moved out of Queens and in with his aunt in Newark."

"Man, that sucks. Well, let's pay this guy a visit, maybe we can make him smile," Aeson said.

"Well, thing is, he can't smile. In fact, I'm pretty sure his mouth, and most of his face were lost in the explosion."

———

The metal cup he handed her was red, and made Katie think of the blood that would have been leaking out his nose if he weren't wearing that badge. She dismissed the thought and sipped the coffee. Her first desire was to throw it in his face. Everything is a weapon if need be, you just have to seize the opportunity to use it. She sipped the hot coffee and purposefully burned her mouth in order to distract herself from the sadistic thoughts she couldn't seem to stop.

"Watch out now, it's hot," the Ranger warned.

"Thanks, it's perfect," she lied, not even wincing as she swished the newly boiled brew around her mouth. "A strong cup of coffee must be perfect to get you going on your hike."

"Usually is, but I'm on a zero day, you know what that is?"

"YES," she responded sternly, upset at the fact that he wouldn't be leaving, and there didn't seem like anywhere else for her to go to park the camper and be close enough to the Zucharino's house, "it's when you sit around all day, patch up your blisters, and try and get friendly with fellow campers." She winked to compliment her last words, just to see his reaction.

Dan, Sergeant Daniel Portman, appeared oblivious to her flirtations. Seduction was just as much a part of Katie's toolkit as was her powerful reverse punch, and she found his lack of response noteworthy.

"Zero day is just a peaceful time to take it all in, reflect on what I've done, and what I'll be doing for the next few months," he told her.

His gear looked weathered, there was dirt underneath his fingernails, and she wished there was a shower somewhere for him to use. "Thanks for the coffee Dan," she said as she looked at his hands for a wedding ring, "does your spouse, or your boy-friend miss you being gone so long?"

Dan turned just a shade lighter than the metal cup she drank from and didn't compose himself before responding, "Oh, I'm not gay, not married either."

"OK Dan, time for me to head in, and do my own reflections, as the doctor ordered. Enjoy your zero day." She handed the cup back to him and disregarding his rank smell whispered into his ear, "Thanks for the coffee."

Locking the door behind her Katie was pleased that she left Dan unbalanced, perhaps even confused; it would now be easier to get the upper hand if necessary. Despite his looks and odor, something about this hiking Ranger was off. If he stayed any longer than he said she would have to act.

———

"This is it, Brunswick St, Building 11, Apartment 43," Han informed Aeson. Han hadn't, in his memory, ever seen an actual apartment building up close. He hadn't been on any streets other than his own, and lived within a private, gated community. The *Inner City* was just a concept to him, only experienced through mass media. When they parked things appeared quiet. It was still morning, and being that it was Friday, most people were out working.

Han stepped off the bike but kept his helmet on. He didn't know at that moment if he was ecstatic or just petrified, but his knees were shaking.

Aeson noticed that Han was standing up extra straight, but was looking around in a paranoid sort of way. He expected his young, sheltered student to be in some type of shock, and was himself terrified at the potential repercussions of what he was guiding Han to do. Aeson never considered himself a big thinker, but he always had to think, and fend for himself. He wanted his client and friend to be able to do the same, and was willing to accept the consequences of breaking his contract to do so.

As Han's personal coach Aeson had been given many warnings, and signed a confidentiality agreement the first day of his employment. The family was convinced paparazzi, crazed fundamentalists, or even Han's own dad, could make life horrible for him. "There are sick people out there," he remembered Grandma Zucharino telling him as she sipped her tea; "And that father of his... forget about it. He's a nut."

Aeson just knew in his gut that this was too important to not do because of fear. A strange music began to echo through the streets and for a split second a chill went up Aeson's spine.

The fighter quickly realized the source of the music and told Han, "It's OK, it's just a sandwich truck." The truck parked at the end of the street and now the middle-eastern music Han had heard blared out.

"Breakfast Filafel!" screamed the man. Suddenly Han's nervous energy took flight. He jumped in panic and ditched it in the alley of Steven's building. Aeson activated the bike's security and followed him.

"It's OK dude," Aeson said, pulling out a pair of Ray Bans and a New York Yankees cap from his motorcycle jacket. "I really don't think anyone's going to notice that you look different, and if they do they're not going to care. But if you're worried just put your sunglasses and baseball hat on like we'd talked about."

Han's black visor pointed at Aeson and slowly his gloved hands rose to the helmet. It lifted an inch, two inches, three, then Han popped the helmet all the way off and pushed it into Aeson's chest. He snatched the hat and glasses from his coach and had them on in seconds.

"You got this Han. You're doing great," encouraged Aeson while looking over his own shoulder, trying hard to not be as nervous as Han was. "All that confidence you have in the VIP room, let it flow, like water."

Han took short quick breaths and whispered the word "Flow." He pushed his back against the wall and felt the bricks through his leather gloves. "I can't go up there, not yet. His aunt will get scared. Steven will understand. Let's just go."

"Look at me Han," Aeson said as he held out his right hand to invite a bro hug. Aeson found it easy to put aside his own fears when it came to helping the kid. "Look at me and take a deep breath. That's it, now exhale slowly." Han's system started to relax and he let Aeson know it by the steadiness of his grip.

"So we came here to just see the outside of his building?" asked Aeson.

"No coach. I'm just not going to use the front door," and with that Han handed his gloves over, then pulled off his sneakers. He turned around, and began to climb the almost sheer brick face. His hands and feet pinched the brick with equal strength, and his agility was unmatched by even the most world class climbers. Aeson suddenly wasn't sure whether to protest or cheer him on. Han moved so smoothly up the wall that Aeson could just look up in awe, mouth agape. Aeson realized that even if people didn't notice Han's unique genetic make-up they might just think the two of them were burglarizing an apartment building. He looked down at the helmet and gloves in his hands, picked up the sneakers, and walked back to the bike. Aeson decided it would be best to wait and try not to attract attention as Han climbed up four floors to visit a friend he met in the virtual gaming world.

Han was up to his destination in seconds, and began to shimmy to the left in order to find Steven's room. The first window he looked in had a baby's crib in it so he kept going. In the next window Han saw someone playing one of his favorite games, *Donnybrook*. The guy's back was turned and his face was covered in an oculus mask, but Han knew he was too mobile to be Steven. It was the third window, apartment 43, where Han found him.

His new friend had described his injuries to him in detail, but nothing could have prepared Han for what he saw.

Han crouched with his hands and feet balanced on the sill. Placing his fingertips against the pane, he pushed, and it slid open. As soon as his foot entered the room a med-care-bot began to move towards him. Its treads made a soft whirring sound on the light brown carpet.

"Han?" an electronic voice asked. Steven's soft thin fingers moved over small sensitive keyboards. "Did you really come through the window? That's so cool."

Chapter 11
A TRICKSTER

The light from the laptop's screen illuminated the back room of the camper. Katie sat cross legged on the open floor, and pushed her sleeping bag aside. The room was without furniture. She assumed it was in the style of a Japanese home. The floor was as soft as a wrestling mat, as were the walls and ceiling. All storage and appliances were hidden within moveable spaces. She could stretch and even stand up to full height if she wanted to. Katie appreciated the open Zen feeling but did not let herself get too comfortable. She tied her hair back and sat up straight.

Han had emailed her early that morning:

I'll be out all day! Want to meet in the Ultimate Underground's bleachers tomorrow night? I hope that didn't sound creepy? My coach is fighting and you can meet my new friend Hephaestos. He's really cool. And yes, you read correctly, I'm actually going out. ☺

What luck! Katie thought. Badgley's going to have to give us what we need.

Katie responded to Han as her on-line twelve year old persona Kat:
See you there Monkey King!

When her email reply was sent she stretched in celebration, then she opened another letter. This time it was from Dr. Jason Badgley. She stopped smiling and felt her jaw tighten again as she read. It was an impersonal series of questions.

Are you establishing a better relationship with him yet?

Is he ready to meet me?

Was it the right move to park an RV and camp so close to the house?

Katie read and re-read the last question half a dozen times. How does he know where I am? She thought to herself. Mr. Senga gave me the keys at the last minute and I haven't been in communication with Badgley. The feeling of someone else having any type of power over her simply enraged her. Dammit! She bit her lip to muffle her swearing.

Katie felt the cool cabin heating up, and realized it was her own anger that was making her sweat. She opened the door for a breath of crisp air. "More coffee? Got plenty," asked Dan with a goofy smile hidden within a mat of red steel wool. She slammed the door shut and slid back into the dimly lit space.

Badgley is having me followed. Me! Who never loses sight of the target. Me! Who always gets the job done. Me! Who would make him wet his pants if he ever gathered up the courage to meet face to face! Me! Me, me... And the best he could get to track me is a smelly, two-bit, amateur.

———

The room was small; not much bigger than Han's VIP space. The walls were yellow and the paint was peeling. There was nothing in terms of decoration; no posters of athletic heroes or panoramic views of far-away cities. Instead it was like a battlefield hospital in a futuristic war-zone.

Steven was prone, bedridden, with the entirety of his insubstantial form shielded by an oxygenated hard plastic covering. Only his two hands, eyes, and forehead were exposed but shadowed beneath geared ledges. The keyboard-activated platforms housed his VIP goggles and two miniature 3-D printers.

"Stand still, please," the robotic voice requested. Han complied and watched as the toy-like med-bot wheeled towards him. "Jesus, you look nervous. And a bit shady with the hat and glasses," it spoke, then paused in realization. "My bad," the voice had changed to a more human and familiar one. "I don't get many visitors," Han's friend from the VIP world, Steven Brutzos explained through the deft movements of his fingertips.

"Yeah it's me," Han paused, not used to filling in silence, "can I move now?"

"Hah! I can't believe it, the Monkey King himself in my own room. Course you can move!" Steven's digits became faster and more animated, which added an excited tone to his computer produced voice.

Han stood awkwardly for another moment and tried not to feel self-conscious. When he moved closer to Steven the whirr of the care-giving robot followed behind him.

"You don't get out much either I'm guessing, or else I would have already known about you. You have probably never seen anything like me before. Well, I've never seen anything like you before. I bought it all, most of it anyway, with money I earned myself."

Perhaps for balance, perhaps for companionship, Han reached out and put his hand on the cold smooth plastic casing. Han theorized about Steven's injuries. He might have had his hands folded on top of his head in a position of surrender just before the claymore, or some other ground based explosive went off at his feet, annihilating everything below his eyes. It's a miracle he survived at all.

"It looks like a casket right? I wanted to get the male model shell but I cheaped out at the last minute."

"VIP code must pay well," commented Han as he moved his hand gently across the life support system's surface and tilted his head to curiously, albeit slowly, examine his friend. Steven was physically far more machine than flesh, and Han tried to imagine what that must be like.

"It's a special skill, requires a different type of genius," Steven said immodestly. "Don't worry Han, from the looks of your Monkey King armor and the way you figured out how to make a useable weapon, I think you got what it takes."

"I'll have your back in the Tunnel, and you teach me how to make a VIP room," said Han, as he looked towards Steven's head. The sight of Steven's face was obstructed by the VIP goggles' platform.

"Shake on it," Steven added, which surprised the still inquisitive but equally concerned Han. Steven's right hand left its sensitive keyboard and carefully extended. There was no arm as far as Han could see, only a soft, brown skinned hand that was opening itself as carefully as a flower does in the early morning sun.

Han kept contact with the life support casing as he carefully pushed his right hand forward to meet Steven's.

Steven felt the thick leathery skin of his human ape hybrid friend. There was no need for conversation. Han was his first real friend since the loss of his family and entire community. Steven suddenly felt as if he were dreaming, for a surge of joy went through his phantom body. And how could this happen except if in a dream?

His left hand moved again and began its soft, efficient communication, as if it were the hand of a master pianist painting a symphony in the air. "Can I look at you Han, with my own eyes?"

"Of course," he replied softly and without hesitation.

The sound of the platform's gears resonated through the small room as Steven typed. The ledge which hung over his head lifted up then moved back. Steven's eyes closed to prepare for the light cast through the window. Han moved closer while keeping his friend's frail palm in his grasp. He gazed upon Steven's closed eyes, and at the top of his head, which still grew feint bits of afro textured hair. Han's heart filled with compassion and he wanted to cry at that moment, but he stayed steady. Han became still but gently smiled so that his eyes would not well up in tears.

———

"Give me a minute Dan!" Katie shouted as she looked in the mirror above the RV's sink. "I'd like that other cup of coffee now. And then I'm going to do some yoga."

Dan's eyes widened as he watched Katie exit her camper wearing yoga pants, a sweater, black leather gloves, and a scarf. She approached him after pushing her blonde hair back in a fleece headband. "Tell me you stretch Dan," she said as she took hold of the metal cup that was steaming and full of potent black coffee.

"Not really, I probably should, but today's…"

"Zero day, c'mon Dan, give me a break. You need a zero day because you don't stretch and exercise properly. Even if you do lose that gut by the time you get across the country, you'll just gain it right back because you don't have good exercise habits. I can tell by your posture," she said, goading Dan to pull his shoulders back and sit up taller. She sat with him, staring intently, only breaking her gaze to drain the mug.

"Let's start with breathing exercises," the now wide awake Katie directed.

"Okay," replied Ranger Dan, who was also awake and beginning to entertain a crazy notion that this woman, who was beautiful in a tough girl sort a way, was interested in him. "Breathing's not too difficult, I'll give it a try," he said then flashed his wittiest smile.

"Watch my stomach," Katie told him while kneeling almost at his feet. Dan watched from a legless camp chair and was reclining back as if he were at home in front of the TV.

"Watching stomach," said Dan. His mouth disappeared entirely within a sponge of facial hair and his eyes found a single focus.

She held her palm over her navel area and puffed out her tight abdominal wall. As her center filled with air she pushed out a muscular pot belly. When she exhaled her abs sucked back in and squeezed her lungs' contents out. Her mouth never opened, only her nostrils, which gave her an even more fierce lioness like countenance. "You see how I did that Dan. Now you try."

Dan eyed her with comical suspicion but did as he was told. His hand rested against his own soft midsection, and as he inhaled his belly moved but certainly didn't take on the rotund proportions it should have. Dan was trying to not reveal just how much mass he put on this past winter before starting his trek. He held his serious gaze but tried to watch Katie in his periphery.

"Good, but try to relax. Here let me help," she said before smoothly rising to one knee then sliding behind him like a college wrestler doing a takedown drill. Katie put her hand over his and said, "Let me feel, push those abs out, good, then exhale and suck that gut in." She pressed her palm hard into his and his wind emptied in one giant gasp. Before he could inhale she quickly placed her free gloved hand over his mouth and pinched his nose shut. Katie continued to apply pressure on his abs while leaning her upper body into the back of his head. It was like some sort of maniacal Heimlich maneuver. Dan appeared as if he was bowing before his eyes closed and he lost consciousness. The last thing he saw was a crow, slowly turning its head side to side and seeming to disapprove of the strange scene that had just unfolded.

———

"Is there anything else modern medicine could do for him?" asked Aeson through the helmet phone as he cruised the streets for Lulu.

"Definitely, but his insurance considers human robot convergence cosmetic and they only pay for life-saving tech," spoke Han grimly.

The same old story thought Aeson as he swallowed bitterly, money. Fantasies coursed through his imagination, and visions of himself as a super successful fighter, one so rich that he could help Han's friend out. "How much do you think convergence surgery would cost?" he asked.

"Before therapy, which would be totally necessary to help him and the technology assimilate, I'd say about fifty million."

Aeson's wheels made a barely noticeable skid as he put on the brakes. "That's a lot of money Han. Just try not to lose hope."

Han was silent, and Aeson wanted to help him. "Is there anything Steven wants that we could get him?"

They both sat on the idling bike wearing their helmets for a minute, as Han thought about what Steven wanted. "He wants to go back to Queens, or at least see it. He misses his old neighborhood and wants to see what life is like now. He thinks the news coverage is all Secular Army propaganda."

"Propaganda?" Aeson questioned as he dismounted his motorcycle.

"Yeah, it's when a government or other power structure purposefully manipulates the..."

"I know what propaganda is Han. It just makes me think of all Lenora's warnings about New York City and why I shouldn't go anywhere near it."

"Yeah but you are near it, and it's our experience," said Han, "so shouldn't we research it?"

Aeson heard Han repeating the words that the Sifu had taught him. They were the same words that Bruce Lee himself had taught the Sifu. "Let's go tomorrow, and we'll bring some helmet cams."

"Sounds good to me," replied Han, almost in disbelief of his new adventurous life. Han moved off of the bike with an exaggerated lift of his leg, as if he were a cowboy who's been on the trail for too long.

Aeson moved on to present matters; "Well, this is where I saw her yesterday. Now I guess we just look around and see if we can find her."

It became a strange scene with Aeson walking around what looked to be a small homeless community's camping area, and Han who followed, still wearing his closed helmet, his gloves, and his jacket zipped up to the neck. Aeson looked back and told Han, "Her name's Lulu, let's both start asking around."

Although it had probably been a cold night, Spring had dawned, and the city's shelters emptied into open fields like the one they were on. Plastic bags, cardboard, and two old tents colored the grounds as if it were the aftermath of some wild concert. Perhaps they were up all night and were now famished for sleep? Perhaps they were like vampires, without their elixir they had to stay shut down. There could have been twenty, or even twenty five of them, strewn about like dolls put in place by a giant child.

Han nodded his helmeted head in agreement with Aeson's search. He noticed two feet sticking out from beneath a cardboard box that was underneath a crab apple tree. He split from Aeson's direction, and his coach gave him a nod that all was OK.

"Excuse me," came out muffled from behind the black visor. "Excuse me!" Han repeated, feeling like he had to shout to be heard. The owner of the blue Nike running sneakers was startled, and then became agitated when he saw how close a masked person was to his own sleeping form.

"Hell you want from me! I'm sleeping. Somebody shaking me down! Community Watch! Community Watch!" he yelled. His panic doubled as Han continued to walk towards him, visor closed, apparently not saying anything. The confusedly fear filled man tore through his shelter's roof, oblivious to Han's apologies that were absorbed by the helmet's protective padding.

Aeson ran over to check out the commotion and quickly realized he wasn't the only one to become alert when the shouting started.

The field's entire population began to rise as if they were the dead becoming reanimated. Han looked around and immediately felt surrounded. He feared that removing his mask would only illicit more panic. "Community Watch Muther F#@%*!" a man pushing a shopping cart towards Han shouted. Behind him stood the stumbling guy in bright blue Nikes, to his left and right were a tall black man and a short Asian woman who danced in place in fighting stances. He had nowhere to go but straight up, so with a simple bending of his knees and a powerful push Han leapt. From the air he saw the zombie like vagrants awakening. Some of them brandished weapons.

The shopping cart plowed into the cardboard shelter but the couple locked down on it to stop its movement. They both gazed up in awe at Han's sixteen foot vertical jump. Han came back down inside the shopping cart and instinctively crouched. As his head popped up the woman screamed and swung her bent fist with lightning speed. She hit Han's helmet with the back of her wrist. To his horror the small Asian woman's blow caused his supposedly indestructible visor to spider web with cracks.

"Lulu! Chill!" the thin tall man shouted. "Let's just take off. There's something weird 'bout this guy."

"No Jay-cob! Nobody shake us down in our own hood!" she angrily replied, the full weight of her painful drug urges transferred into skillfully delivered violence.

"Lulu?" questioned Aeson, just before some buzzing inside his head told him to look over his shoulder. A baseball bat, its aluminum surface dented and dirty was swinging through the air and heading straight at his skull. It whistled as it passed over him and crunched as it made contact with a tree. As Aeson rose he saw Han who looked like he was stuck in a shopping cart. His visor was smashed and he was surrounded by people who were preparing to dish out lethal force. An explosion went off inside him when he thought of the danger he had put the twelve year old in. Han was a special twelve year old who wasn't in fact supposed to leave his house. The bat reversed its course but Aeson stayed low and swept the back of his legs out from under him with a driving shin. "Ahhhh!" the batter shouted as he crumbled.

Han placed both his hands on the cart and easily sprang out and away from the small but powerful helmet smashing lady. She turned her head, screamed something in Chinese, and took chase. Aeson moved forward but was swarmed suddenly. He elbowed a guy who tried to grab both his ears, crumbling him instantly. A glass bottle soared through the air and Aeson snapped out a front kick and shattered it to pieces. A side-kick sent a would-be tackler butt first into the tree.

Han wanted to get on all fours and run. He stayed tall though, and kept himself masked, even though his vision was now obstructed. Aeson could see as he defended himself Han awkwardly trying to circle the field to get back to the bike.

What was I thinking, expecting a drug addict to help the kid I'm supposed to be helping! Aeson screamed inside at himself as the man he kicked collapsed clutching at his abdomen.

A sharp pain wrapped his lower leg. A chain struck while Aeson's back was turned and constricted tightly as someone pulled. Aeson's leg began to drag as two others took hold of his arms. A fourth man who looked like an ex-football player, tackled Aeson's supporting leg. He began to fall in disbelief of what was happening. He kept his eyes on Han though, and as he lost his balance he witnessed Lulu crouch low, leap, spin, and kick towards Han's head. "No!" Aeson shouted before finding strength in his core. He straightened so that the cluster could not pin him down. His feet dug in and he started seeing everything in black and white just before he went berserk. The men holding his wrists were rammed together, and the guy with the chain was now eating dirt. The football tackle ended badly. A downward elbow to the dorsal spine rendered him useless.

The small sneakered foot of Lulu made contact just under the chin of Han's helmet. The force sent the protective covering up and off his head. The black helmet soared through space and all eyes followed. As it crashed to the ground everyone's attentions turned towards who was underneath.

Aeson was knocking the wind out of people with single blows to the midsections as he marched towards the scene, committed to annihilating anyone who would lay a hand on the kid. He just wanted to get Han his helmet and get the hell out of Newark.

Han stood and it seemed like it was the first time that air from somewhere other than his family's house had touched his face. He saw what Lulu was capable of but suddenly felt unafraid. He looked towards his coach and saw fifteen or so people cradling their stomachs on the ground around him.

"No more Aeson!" Han put his hands up and shouted. All eyes were riveted on this ape like creature who could speak. "This isn't right! They're freaking out because they think we're attacking them!"

Aeson pulled back a punch that was going to send another to the ground. He realized he was panting. Color began to return. His opponents were as Han had noticed, decrepit and in need of help, not a beat down. They were just guarding their turf. But what about Lulu? Is she going to really start to fight now?

Lulu wasn't fighting anymore however. She was kneeling. "Sun Wukong," she whispered, "Sun Wukong." The whole field slowly approached the scene, saw Lulu's reverence, and kneeled to the now helmetless Han Zucharino. "Sun Wukong," was all Lulu could say.

———

"Hey Dan I have your bosses on the phone. Didn't you say you work for the Office of the Interior? Here I'll let you talk," Katie said as she approached Dan Portman who was still in his camp chair.

"So you're saying he doesn't work with you guys and never has? Got it. OK. Can you explain that to him because he's going around to female campers and flashing his shiny gold park ranger badge. Here," Katie said before placing her phone at Dan's ear. Dan could not take hold of the phone for his arms were tied behind his back. He tried to tell them that yes he was an imposter but the woman who was holding the phone was plum crazy. He tried to tell them that he was the one who needed help, but only gagging whimpers came out. The bandana stuffed into his mouth impeded all communication. He feared that if he kept trying to speak he would choke, and the mad woman who tied him up would do nothing but watch him die.

"Thank you for your time sir," said Katie into the phone. She hung up and shook her head back and forth at Dan in disapproval. "Well Dan, if that is your real name. Badgley has gotten sloppy hiring someone like you. I bet you never really wanted to get into this line of work. You probably enlisted and got picked up by a security firm before you could even properly fire a weapon."

Dan's eyes opened wide in disbelief at the beautiful but frightening person before him. He wished he had just left her alone, and that he was back on the trail, acting cool and important with his fake badge and big beard.

"You'll have time to re-think your life Dan." With that she dragged him by the back of his camp chair into his tent. As she zipped it up she looked in, smiled, and said, "Thanks for the coffee."

———

"You don't have to kneel Lulu," Han spoke.

Lulu looked up in astonishment. The deity she prayed to every day, no matter how badly she shook or how high on Synthetic Synergy she was had chosen to materialize and speak with her. She smiled, and buried her head to hide her joyful lack of self-control.

"Will you meet us at the dojang? We want to train with you. Aeson is my coach and he thinks your style of Kung-Fu would fit my body type."

Her god was a trickster, and she wondered but didn't question what he was up to. Lulu flexed her jaw so as not to burst into excited laughter. Her eyes opened wide as she said, "Of course Sun-Wukong. It will be an honor."

"I brought the … stuff you wanted. Last time you told me we could do a trade. These pills for…" Aeson was not liking the role he was playing, but got caught up in it nonetheless. He was shocked when Lulu rejected his offer. In fact she became angry at even the mention of it.

"No! I don't need chemicals anymore. You fool."

Han helped her up and looked at Aeson with a half-smile. "You know where it is right?" Han asked her.

"Meet you there!" Lulu cried gleefully and took off running.

———

Dr. Jason Badgley rewound the footage of Katie interrogating some poor tied up man. He thought, my God she's insane, they're both insane.

He began to type into his phone:

Stella. I made a terrible mistake. Keep Han in your sights, and keep him safe.

———

Hi Han. I'm looking forward to tomorrow night and meeting your friend. I'm planning on bringing a friend too!

Katie sent Han a text then decided she would see what else she could find out about Badgley.

As she approached the tent she could hear his suppressed cries. What was he saying? He keeps repeating the same thing.

Dan had a single word sounding off in a perpetual loop, "Cklowe." Just as his captor had recommended Dan had done some thinking. He regretted his actions yes, but her situation, he felt, after giving it considerable attention in his harried thoughts, had really come down to one thing, the crow. Before he passed out there was a large black bird turning its head mechanically and watching. The whole time he sat in that camp chair, lazy as a stuffed buzzard, he sipped his coffee and watched that crow watching the RV. Whenever the woman came out the crow's eyes followed her. It was locked on to her, but whenever she looked at it the big black bird just hopped away.

"What are you saying Dan?" Katie asked, now dragging him out.

"Cklowe! Ahh Cklowe!"

"What's that?" she asked again, this time removing the moist cloth from out of his palate.

"The crow," he said no longer screaming. "Don't look. Every time you look at it, it bolts."

"Dan. If you're trying to trick me, or do whatever you do to people you meet in the woods know that..." before she could finish her sentence she caught site of something in the mirrored surface of his stainless steel coffee kettle. It was the very bird Dan was talking about. She shushed him from continuing and slowly picked up the red metal mug he offered to guests. Katie's eyes focused on the image of the bird but also let go of predicting its precise location and distance. She didn't have time for calculating as her head turned with lightning speed. Both her eyes stayed open as she exhaled and let the projectile weapon fly. Her shoulder whipped her arm, and she released the sturdy cup. It smashed into the bird's throat and sent it toppling down in a feathery clump.

———

No one was in the dojang, as Sifu said, but they still used the dimly lit back room. Lulu shed about eight layers and stood up to align her skeleton and stand with her feet shoulder width apart. As her hands raised to eyelevel she dropped into a squat. Han and Aeson mimicked. Jacob sat against the wall sipping a shake that Aeson had given him.

With each move, each sway of a limb, strike to the air, or roll on the ground, Han felt at ease, natural, and more powerful. Aeson struggled to keep up but didn't mind slowing down to watch Han perform so perfectly. Soon Lulu would have to stop and watch as the very special twelve year old repeated the leaping, rolling, mischievous and mighty Monkey style of Kung-Fu.

Chapter 12
ADVENTURE IS AN UNDERSTATEMENT

"Pop, it's Stella. I'm at the store, is Han there? He's not answering his phone."

"He's in the gym. Kid loves to train. Been at it all morning," said Grandpa, simply going off the sounds of pads being hit and grunts that he heard. The glass doors of their home gym were fogged up, just what should happen during a hard workout.

Meanwhile in Newark, Han was training, and seemed to master Monkey Flies Into the Sky, Iron Wall, and Attacking Iron Wall; techniques that took Lulu half her childhood to learn correctly. Han kept going, and flowing, and seemed, once he had committed to muscle memory the advanced forms that Lulu had performed, to begin creating his own.

Aeson heard a "Ding! Ding! Ding!" sound and jumped up in attention, he looked around as if he was one of Pavlov's fighters who just heard his signal to start swinging.

"It's my new ring-tone coach," Han said, briefly pausing with only his fingertips supporting him in a one armed pushup position. "Sorry, can you check it?"

"Sure," Aeson said, calming down and wiping the sweat from his brow and hands before going into Han's jacket pocket. "Dude," said Aeson to Han.

Han paused again, this time with his arms at his sides and balanced perfectly the crown of his head! "Who was it?"

"Your mom! And she says she's going to be home in less than an hour. She's got to talk with you; she said it's about your father."

"My...?" and with that Han lost his composure and crumbled to the floor.

Jacob commented as he slurped down the last of his shake, "Oooh... that looked like it hurt Monkey King."

———

Jason Badgley paced back and forth within the confines of his laboratory, inside his fortress like house in upstate New York. Several computer terminals were open. He watched helplessly as Katie's gloved hand gripped the head of his unconscious bird. All went dark and Dr. Badgley felt fear course up and down his spine.

He opened his desk drawer and retrieved a small digital picture frame. He watched as a series of photos scrolled by. His favorite, the one he always paused for, was taken in India in a great valley in the Himalayas. Hanuman Zucharino Badgley was six months old and was cradled by both his mother Stella and by his father Jason. Everyone was smiling. He remembered the Buddhist monk who took the picture. He was on pilgrimage from Japan and appeared overjoyed to have met their special baby.

If only they could have stayed in Uttarakhand forever? If only they never found him? What-ifs were a pipe dream and the forces that conspired against them were great. By nightfall of the very same day that the sweet picture was taken they had come for them. Dr. Jason Badgley would be forced to become an indentured scientist, serving the often unethical and dark wishes of his kidnappers. Han and his mother would be allowed to reside in America and to enter a type of self-imposed house arrest; one that would last for over twelve years.

The frame shook in his hand before he returned it to the closed draw-er. He picked up his car keys and prepared to act; not as a servile scientist anymore but as a father.

———

Han and Aeson thanked Lulu, offered payment again, then locked up the dojang and headed for home. Almost as soon as they exited Newark proper they were in traffic. "Can't you go faster," Han beckoned.

"If we get pulled over Han your Mom is going to find out." Now is not the time to be taking even bigger risks, right?" Aeson tried to explain things to his worried protégé but Han's grip on Aeson's back just became more tense. "But then again what's life without risks." He lifted his chin and yanked back on the handlebars. The front tire came off the ground as Aeson accelerated.

The fighter's move would have sent Han spilling off backwards if he wasn't so strong. Instead of becoming angry or afraid Han shifted into pure excitement. "Yeeeee!" he screamed as the front wheel came back down with a bounce and they began to weave in and out of lethargic automobiles.

Aeson blasted the old style rock and roll music that his dad listened to then revved the engine again. With every opening left by cars parting they sped up, and with every stalemate they cut the line. Han let go of his coach and raised his arms in a gesture of invincibility. The taste of free-dom was incredible.

———

Dan's hope in the truth freeing him stayed alive even when Katie broke the large bird's neck with her bare hands. The noise that signaled the end of the winged creature's life sickened Dan and he felt as if even though he was bound in his camp chair, that he were on a very rocky boat ride. He convinced himself that now that this madwoman had found her spy she would let him go. What Katie Carouche did next nearly extinguished his last small flame of optimism. She began to squeeze, and squeeze, and squeeze on the dead creature's neck. And as the head separated from the body she laughed saying, "Pop goes the... camera!" The headless black mass thumped to the ground as she wound her arm back and threw the head over the cliffs and into the rocks that overlooked the Hudson River. Dan Portman tried not to think about what kind of person gets tracked by a bio-engineered bird and hoped that if she didn't untie him, at least she would get rid of the decapitated bleeding mass that lay at his feet.

———

Stella and her mother sat in their car on the Garden State Parkway. "All these people going out to lunch," Grandma Zucharino said with banality, innocently trying to fill in a void that was created by her ex son-in-law's text message.

"It's noon-day traffic Ma, nothing new," Stella replied with enough snap to hurt. Almost immediately she reflected on her sharp response. "I didn't mean to get smart with you Ma. It's just that even though we knew this day would come eventually, it doesn't seem real. I'm just..."

"Worried. I know Stell, me too. Jason was a good man when you met him. He just got in with the wrong people."

"Jason doesn't contact me in so long and now he does and, and, it's like he was really concerned for Han's safety."

"You kidding me. The house has the best security system around. Jason designed it specifically to protect his son."

"You're right Ma. I guess I just want to see Han, you know. We've sheltered him for so long. I'm worried he's not ready."

"We did what we had to do Stella. And he'll be ready for whatever comes his way. He's a Zucharino. And the Zucharinos are fighters."

———

The cars started to speed up and Aeson's own fears began to decline. "Han, I think we're almost there. But just in case can you check the web for a faster route?"

"Already on it," Han said in reply. After half a minute Han had the shortcut. "Garden State Parkway will get us there in five minutes instead of ten. Take this exit!"

"Well then Garden State Parkway here we come!"

Han's map search didn't say anything about more traffic on the Parkway, or about his mother and grandmother occupying one of the sluggishly rolling vehicles. Han looked around interestedly at all the different faces and to his horror noticed a car that looked identical to his mom's coming up on their left. He kept staring into the windows of this somewhat typical white sedan, hoping to relieve himself of anxiety and even laugh off the obviously unwarranted fear that was shortening his breath.

As his eyes focused on the passenger side he saw the unmistakable form of Milly Zucharino, his grandmother. Han jerked backwards with such force that Aeson had to tell his bike to "Right yourself!" Han could see her doing a double take on Aeson and himself, turning towards Stella, then turning back to look at them. His heart began pounding. How could he have been so stupid as to jeopardize his coach's job! Aeson didn't know all the reasons behind his own student's planned isolation, and probably didn't understand the true impact of the documents he signed. Han's eyes stayed glued to the back of Grandma's head. As she began to turn towards the two of them Han made what he thought was the best possible move. He pushed his hands on the seat beneath him and leapt backwards onto the cargo wagon of the semi behind them.

"Han?" Aeson inquired, suddenly feeling lighter and faster. "Han, is that your mom's car?"

Han was still communicating through the helmet phone, "Yeah, it is. Don't worry, if they make eye contact just wave."

"But? Han..."

"I'm not on the back of the bike anymore coach."

Aeson turned quickly as if he were shocked by a tap on the shoulder in a dark room. The bike made a radical dip towards its left. "Right yourself!" Aeson hollered.

The bike popped back up and at the same time Grandma Zucharino's window went down. He at least had been spotted.

"Aeson! Let them take the Alpine exit and we'll keep going. I'll jump back on the bike when they're gone!" Han yelled as he clung, stomach down, to the hood of the freight vehicle.

Grandma was still staring at Aeson in wonder as they turned off.

The traffic broke and cars began to accelerate. "Han! You still there man?"

The truck was getting into the faster lane when Han made his move. He wanted to hop as lightly as possible to the roof of a van before telling Aeson to slow down so he could climb off. The cracked visor was confusing his perception though and when he jumped he did not account for the van speeding up. He barely made it onto the bumper and his head smacked hard into the back doors. His visor's damage was made worse and visibility was almost zero. The mask wouldn't lift up because something had broken. Aeson was nowhere in sight and the highway had quickly become a ninety mile an hour raceway. He climbed to the top but it was like walking in a snowstorm, he couldn't see more than five feet in front of him. This time he didn't think. Panic took over and he removed the helmet and chucked it into the scraggly tree line. Aeson was equally as panicked and began weaving in and out again, this time looking back for his student with each shift in body weight. "Han! Han! You there man?"

The bike's weight suddenly shifted and Aeson began to lose control. He didn't have to direct it this time. The motorcycle's computer took over and straightened things out.

"Han!" Aeson shouted, almost letting his emotion turn to rage. He wanted to double back and drive in the opposite direction to find the kid. Before his mad plan could become reality he felt hands grip his shoulders.

"Dude! Calm down!" Han screamed into the wind. "Just get us home!"

———

Katie went back and forth from sitting in front of the laptop screen to walking the perimeter of the campsite. Now he knew where she was and that was more important than her tying up some Forest Ranger imposter. She had put Dan back in his tent and decided to focus on her real mission, bringing her husband back to life.

Han, you there? How was your day out? Any adventures?

She waited anxiously for his reply. The screen saver activated for lack of activity. She thought about calling Mr. Senga to ask about her Majstro and to inquire as to what other secrets his high tech camper might hold. The screen brightened and she dismissed everything save for the message in front of her.

"Adventure" is an understatement. Han typed as he slipped into workout shorts and a t-shirt from the hamper. "Hey mom! Hey grandma! You guys are home early."

"Han, honey! Is Aeson with you?" His mother asked.

"He had to run out but should be home soon!"

What do you mean Han? Sounds fun. I want in.

Let's put it this way Kat, tomorrow morning we're going to do it again. This time it's Queens.

That sounds awesome! But isn't Queens Secular Army territory now?

It's risky, but that's part of the experience.

So cool.

Just before sundown Badgley pulled in to Katie's campsite. He didn't really think she would be there but he came prepared with a long range tazer of his own design.

The only thing he found in the camp was the body of his bio-engineered bird. He sat on the ground thinking about how he was going to remedy this bad situation and decided that he would break from the protocol and end the silence, tomorrow.

In the morning he would finally explain himself to his ex-wife. In the meantime Katie Carouche was a loose cannon, but Katie's husband Majstro was an important client he had to maintain to keep his own cover. Dr. Badgley as a double agent had to keep Majstro alive at all costs but had sworn to his true overseers that he would never let him wake up again.

Resolve filled him and he stood as darkness fell. The moon was quickly rising over the river and he decided it would be worth it to take a look. He thought that because of the way that things were unfolding after tomorrow he may not have too many more peaceful moments. Dr. Badgley stood at the cliff's edge, the enormity of the George Washington Bridge, the historic river below, and the teeming metropolis that stood before him, helped to lighten his concerned mood. He would find a motel for the night, somewhere close by, get some sleep, and make himself presentable for the morning.

As he took in the picturesque view one last time he looked down, following the blue light that was reflecting off the water. His gaze settled at the base of the cliffs and a cluster of trees. What he saw in the tangle gave rise to the same terror that had filled him when he watched his crow die, only it was worse. A man's dead eyes stared up at him, his thick beard matted in blood. One of the man's legs had broken so intensely that it had become misplaced above his own head. A hefty branch had punctured his abdomen. He hoped he died quickly.

Fear rose up and crashed over Dr. Badgley like a leviathan who emerged from the waters below. He stumbled backwards and began nervously testing his weapon. It lit up the camp with bright electric bolts and cast an eerie illumination over the large decapitated bird.

———

Katie was almost there, and hoped the good doctor would be home to let her in. She wanted to be able to talk to him face to fist. She rang the gate's bell, when no one answered she turned to retrieve a few items she found concealed within the vehicle's tire jack. On the passenger seat sat a thermal lance, which she would use to burn through anything that she could not climb over or crawl through, a few electromagnetic tetsu-bishi, spiked balls that stopped most robots in their tracks, and finally a handful of throwing stars, whose weight gave her the impression that they did more than just poke or cut.

Performing an old fashioned break in might set off an alarm and any number of security measures Badgley had installed, which although not ideal, were not completely threatening. She was quite sure that the doctor would not link his house to any public law enforcement agency. He simply had too many underground clients, and many of their projects were locked away in that lab of his. The only thing she had to worry about was bodily injury, or maybe loss of life, two things she had not only dealt with many times before but were things that gave any job the extra motivation she liked.

Before melting any metal or doing anything drastic like ramming the barrier she decided to take the vehicle back far enough to be out of camera range. Her phone had several black market apps on it that her husband had installed for her before his change. One of them, *Watch Watch Dog*, indicated the presence of cameras that were live and within fifty feet. She climbed to the RV's roof and stared into *Watch Watch Dog's* data field. Eyes were everywhere, but not above the large gate. She began to secure anything that could fall off of her. She stood at the back of the vehicle's roof and began to run. She hit her jump and the camper disappeared beneath her. She realized too late that she wasn't going to clear the spikes. She was glad she used high jump form, and happier still that she was wearing a Kevlar vest beneath her black fleece. Her back met the foot long spikes but before she could become stuck she continued her momentum and thrust both feet in the air. She only made contact for a split second before landing safely on her feet. She immediately looked at her screen and rolled into a clear area. She reached back and felt an inch deep hole in her vest just above her vertebrae. She smiled and adrenaline pumped through her body.

———

"So my dad is really coming over?" Han asked with his mouth full of pancake.

"Well Han, he's a very private person. He'd actually like to meet with me and grandma first..."

"To discuss the custody stuff?" Han asked matter-of-factly.

"Yes Han, to discuss the custody stuff. You have nothing to worry about sweetie. No matter what happens, at thirteen it's..."

"It's my choice, I know Mom. And I'm not worried."

Everyone else clearly was. Grandma must have folded her napkin ten times. Stella was on her third cup of coffee. Granpa wasn't sleeping, Al's mouth had stayed busy with all the extra food he made, and Sal, well, Sal showed his anxiety with his lack of sensitivity to the situation; "You ready for the big fight tonight Aeson?"

No one knew exactly what to say so Sal continued. "Al and I got a surprise for the fighter. Let's call it a bonus for all the great work you've done with the kid. We've got to pick it up from a guy in Brooklyn actually in a little bit."

"Thanks Al, thanks Sal, you guys are too kind to me," Aeson said, slightly skeptical about the uncles' gift.

Han looked up stealthily at Aeson and communicated something with his eyes. Aeson responded by slowly shaking his head and mouthing the words "NO WAY," to him.

Breakfast finished and Han offered to do the dishes; "You guys gotta go. Coach and I got this. Right coach?"

"Of course," Aeson responded, not liking what he suspected Han was up to.

Han hugged his grandmother and mother as they prepared to meet with Jason at a local diner. "Something's different about you Han," his mother noted, "I know this is a lot for you to take in, but ..."

"Ma, I'm almost a teenager remember?"

"Right, almost. Well we'll be back later, and we'll have your father with us."

"Can't wait," Han said with a smile on his poker face as he closed the door behind them. Al and Sal had already left. Aeson started on the dishes and tried to ignore what he knew was coming.

"Let's go coach! I found another helmet! And cameras!"

"But you're going to meet your dad today Han, for like the first time. Don't you want to stay home and, and, get ready?"

"Seriously coach. This is even more reason for us to go. If he comes back into the picture I might not see the outside of house again until I'm eighteen."

Aeson put the wet rag down, closed his eyes and wondered to himself, what have I done?

———

"Steven! We're on our way to Queens!" Han shouted as they neared the great cable bridge. Han's latest helmet was all black with the white silhouettes of Playboy bunnies on either side. It was Sal's old helmet. "I've got you hooked in to both our helmets for communication. We have cams on, so you can toggle between perspectives if you want."

"Han. Dude. This is really cool what you're doing."

"Don't thank me yet Steven," Han replied.

Steven began to see the sun coming up over the water for the first time since the Queens Jihad. Boats passed underneath the bridge. There were plenty of cars to look at and people to see as they approached the city which Steven knew so well and loved so much.

"Steven, hey, it's Aeson here,"

"What's up? You're Han's coach. Thanks for doing this."

"No problem, my pleasure, hey, do you mind if I switch channels when I talk with Han, I don't want things to get to muddled."

"Do whatever you got to do coach."

"Thanks."

Aeson switched channels, "Han! Look, Newark was one thing, but at least it was still in New Jersey. Not only are we going to New York but Queens used to be a war zone, literally!"

"Coach," Han answered in a calm voice, "I know this whole thing is kind of crazy, but Steven needs this man, he's hurting, and I know this is risky but I think it can make a big difference."

Aeson's heart strings pulled and he felt torn between responsibilities. "Isn't there footage of his old neighborhood we could find on-line?"

"Of course coach, but it's not the same. And this isn't just for Steven. Who knows what custody agreements are going to happen between my mom and dad. I could end up living in Timbuktu soon."

"Where's Timbuktu?"

"It's in West Africa, but, that was just a saying, the point is…"

"I get the point dude," Aeson said as they crossed the centerline of the massive overpass. "Let's do this."

———

Katie had a long rough night, and her bandaged back, forearms, and legs testified to that. She hoped she had what she needed and was now making her way back to the small apartment where her husband lay waiting. Stay focused, stay focused, she told herself, think big picture, long term. She activated her phone from the dashboard and called the connection she had made in New Jersey.

"Hello, this is Walter. This the lady who fights like a man?"

"The very same."

Katie as always made sure to do her homework. She had worked with Walter and his thugs before Aeson even arrived on the East Coast. She had paid him to rough Aeson up, to scare him out of taking the coaching job, but Aeson proved too tough. She was no stranger to criminal elements, and knew that Walter would want to prove himself again, not only for the money, but for the criminal pride and reputation that was at stake.

"I'm on it. We got guys posted at the head of the Queensborough and the Tribourough."

"Hang on," she told him as she began to type on the screen in front of her with her free hand.

Hey Han! Did you cross the state line yet! Was the GW what you expected?

Han could see the email go across his helmet screen and was filled with even more energy and confidence when he realized it was Kat, the very girl he wanted to ask out.

Just crossed over. Han voice-typed. It was amazing!

The Queensborough won't be as nice.

We're taking the Tribourough next. Steven wants us to head straight to his old neighborhood in Astoria.

Sweet! See you tonight!

"Move you and your guys to the Triborough Bridge Walter. He's on a motorcycle."

Chapter 13
WALK TALL AND MOVE SLOW

The digital banner above the toll booth read: **Religion is only the illusory Sun which revolves around man as long as he does not revolve around himself**. An image of a bearded man preaching from a book and standing on the deck of a gunship continued to scroll across the banner behind the words. Just before it disappeared off the ticker tape it turned around quickly to restart only to get pushed back down by the gliding slogan. A majestic series of bright suns followed, each bearing the word **BONVENA**.

"Propaganda," Aeson whispered.

"Karl Marx," Han informed.

"I knew that."

"Bonon matenon, good morning," the officer at the window said to Aeson.

"Morning," he pulled up his visor and smiled. She was wearing head to toe flexible body armor and an electronic dog patrolled back and forth around her booth. The woman's straight black hair, and the way she spoke told Aeson she was a SAM from Japan.

"The nature of your visit? I see that this vehicle has never entered Queens before."

"Well... we're... doing some sightseeing, and..."

"And we want to see the Peace Monument!" shouted Han through Aeson's earpiece, "Just say it coach, Steven told me to tell you."

"Peace Monument," Aeson smiled. The guard was a Secular Army Marshall, and part of the largest private peace keeping force on Earth. The army was created by the world economy's wealthiest tech and pharma companies and had dual headquarters in the U.S. and in Japan. They came by invite only but when they showed up their ideology came with them.

"Are you carrying any contraband? Illegal drugs or religious pamphlets?"

"No, no ma'am, no drugs no bibles."

"What?" said Steven to Han, which made Han laugh. His communication was still open so Aeson could hear and feel his protégé cracking up. He was mad for a split second before the giggling began to spread into his own body. Han kept repeating Aeson's comment between giggling; "No ma'am, no drugs no bibles." Aeson clenched his jaw but suddenly felt like he was going to burst with utter immature silliness.

"Is there something funny sir?" she asked. Her sunglasses hid most of her emotions but her tone demanded respect.

"No, no mam," Aeson barely squeezed out as Han's shaking body was making it increasingly difficult to hold it together, "we're just happy to finally be here."

"Very good then, enjoy your stay."

As they drove away the laughter exploded and Aeson could barely get out his command to "Right yourself!"

———

Stella and Milly Zucharino walked into the Tenafly diner and began to immediately search the room for Jason.

"We're meeting someone, Dr. Jay..."

"Right here! Already got a booth right over in the corner," came a voice from behind the two ladies. Alarm quickly changed to curiosity as mother and daughter followed the man who they were supposed to meet.

He was wearing a sweatshirt with the hood up and sunglasses covered his eyes. There was a plate full of fruit peels, cores, and seeds. Jason ordered tea and coffees and everyone settled in, staring at each other, hearts racing.

"You look amazing, both of you. You take all those supplements you sell?"

"Usually only the ones I design," answered Stella with a flinch of her lip that may have been the beginning of a smile.

"You were always a brilliant bio-chemist Stella," Jason said, as his hands lifted and rested on the table, as if magnetism was pulling them closer to his ex-wife's.

"You... you look good too," Stella replied.

"What'ya mean Stell? Ya can't even see him," said Grandma, "he's covered up like the invisible man."

"Ha!" Jason laughed and put his hands on top of theirs. Grandma felt his skin was strange, different, not warm enough but not cold and clammy, like it was a fake hand.

Stella recognized that she was being touched by a strong leathery appendage, much like her son's in feel but not in appearance. As Han came into her thoughts she yanked her hand out of his saying, "Twelve years Jason. I haven't seen you in twelve years."

"Stella, Milly, there's no good way to do this. It's the only way I knew of to keep Han, and you guys, safe."

Jason sat up taller and slid back on his seat. His shoulders opened and he took his hood down and put his glasses on the table.

"Huh..." Milly gasped. Stella put her hands in the prayer position and covered her mouth, as if to shush herself.

"The development didn't start until a year after we were separated," he began to explain.

"Did you know before you guys conceived?" asked Grandma with a gentle sternness and a matter-of-factness that could make one think that she had been waiting twelve years to ask it.

"No! Of course not. I thought it was a failed experiment before Stella and I... fell in love. I would have never risked any of this, not for science, not even for..."

Stella could not break her gaze from the man before her, and nodded like someone who was already privy to this information. The man she once loved was intelligent, bookishly handsome, and had the most optimistic view of science and the world that she had ever known; but could he be trusted?

Now she looked at someone who at first glance appeared paranoid and terrifyingly ugly. His features were partially simian, but only partially. His brow was raised and gave him a Neanderthal like appearance. His teeth were mismatched and a huge fang pushed out of the side of his mouth. His ears were sagging radar dishes that unfolded when his hood came down. His hair had receded strangely enough but had grown thick and black below his cheeks and above his eyes.

Milly took his hand back, this time into both of hers, and felt it as if it were a fabric she was thinking about sewing with.

"It's synthetic Milly, did it myself actually. The experiments turned my muscles without addressing my bones or tendons; my body started to tear itself apart."

"Is this going to happen to Han?" Stella blurted.

"As far as my analysis goes no, Han is a complete hybrid, unlike me. He's transgenetic, the simian and human traits were passed on to him at conception, unlike me, who introduced them into myself. My body will always be in resistance while his will only become more unified."

"How do you live like this Jason? The pain, the secrecy?"

"I kept myself alive even when I wanted to die from the agony."

"Because if you died..." Stella said, "they'd have come back for Han and me."

"Yes," answered Jason as both women clutched his two different hands in theirs.

———

"Ditch your heaters fellas. They got gun sniffers at each booth," instructed Walter to his gang of three. They put pistols in a messenger bag and had the fourth rider make a u-turn and drive away with them. Walter held up his hand that was still in a cast from his last encounter with Aeson. His gang looked at it with enmity in their eyes as they tightened their gloves and adjusted their leather gear. "This is the same guy who stomped you all in our own hood so you can lay it on heavy. The kid we snatch, inject, and ride away with; strapped to my bike. Got it!"

"Got it!" The three of them rolled out from beneath the billboard's shadow and set after their quarry.

Han looked around and was amazed by the order and cleanliness of it all. Queens was not the New York City he expected. There were no homeless people loitering, no loud music blaring from uninsured vehicles, and absolutely not a single religiously affiliated building or house of worship. "Pull over here, please. This is where my mom's church was," Steven told them both.

They dismounted and walked up to investigate. "Take off your helmets. Dang guys, you look like something out of a Bruce Lee movie, walking around all bad with your visors down."

Han tried to explain, "But Steven, thing is..."

"Take off the damn helmet man and move the camera to your collar. Remember what happened in Newark. You scared that poor homeless guy half to death."

Aeson immediately pulled his up and off, then he looked at Han. "Told you. Just put on your hat and sunglasses, this is New York baby."

"You've been hanging out with Sal too much, but, OK." And then he did it, just like that, he was out in public as his true self.

Han looked around for a memorial stone or something to match the site with Steven's memory. As they got closer Han leaned over to a sign so that his friend could see it clearly. It read: SECULAR MEDITATION CENTER Come harmonize with the universal frequency of peace.

"What! That's messed up. That church was here since before the Great Depression, built by immigrants. Faithful immigrants like my mom."

"Sorry man. Do you want us to go into this building?" asked Han.

"No, forget it. How about you guys get some gyros and I'll watch you eat."

"Hah!"

BOOM!

"What the hell was that?" questioned Steven immediately.

"Sounded like a car backfiring," suggested Aeson.

"Look around coach," reminded Steven, "there are strict emissions laws in SAM country. Nothing here can backfire."

Sirens began to wail and a robotic hound that must have been stealthily patrolling the street they were on burst from behind a recycling bin and ran with eyes lit red towards the explosion.

Another sound suddenly came into the picture. It was the noise Aeson heard every time he revved his bike's engine. Han turned away from the silver dog to see three motorcycles charging hard straight at them. The riders were swinging what looked like weighted chains.

"Holy Shit!" Steven exclaimed, "Do something!"

———

"Have you got the full treatment this time?" Mr. Senga asked after a quick bow.

"I think so, the RV is full of gear I took from his lab." Katie had snatched everything that was labeled or near a label that had her husband's name on it.

Katie didn't know the difference between liposomes, plasmid vectors, or protoplast fusion. It was Senga who decided to go with the ballistic DNA injection.

Nothing happened for a long while, which gave them both time to research the treatments and to discuss what Katie did and what their next steps would be. The two had not seen his nostrils reawaken, his fingers become animate, or his eyes at last open. It was his first words that yanked them out of their busy efforts. "Badgley," a scratchy voice whispered, "we need to find Badgley."

———

The spinning chains were called *manriki gusari* and they were a gift from Miss Carouche. She even showed them how to conceal them within the bike's mechanics so that not even one of the SAM's dogs could sniff them out. The explosive element they used as a distraction was known as a *battery bomb*, another one of Katie's easily concealable gifts.

Han was frozen in fear from the sight of the three sinister riders. This wasn't the VIP world where he could just push the door open and blip away from danger. This was what everyone had warned me about he thought, this is why I'm supposed to stay home. The panic began to rise into his throat. Suddenly his excitement about all the new happenings in his life faded. One of the manriki were let-go, and flung, spinning towards Aeson's bare head. Han's mind protected itself by receding into the other aspect of his genetic code. He hurled his helmet at the oncoming marauders and let out a primal scream.

———

"Han! Honey, we're home," Stella announced, trying hard to swallow her anxiety.

"He must be in the cave, he loves it down there," said Grandma.

"Oh yeah, what's he into?" Jason asked.

"The VIP room, it's like a virtual physical experience," Stella explained.

"Oh I know what it is. We, the original group, worked with it, after hacking into the military's virtual training manuals."

"You've really branched out from strictly genetics work. I mean, virtual reality programming and, and you're prosthetic is so..."

"Functional," Jason said finishing Stella's sentence. "Yeah well like our son, the bonobo genes have magnified my ability to mimic. When I wanted to understand surgery, I just watched a video."

"You guys want me to get Han?" Grandma asked.

The two looked at each other and spoke in chorus, "No let him play."

The three of them were silent in indecision until Jason spoke, "We can take this time to discuss security. Let Han get his energy out. We'll meet soon enough."

They discussed the outdoor cameras, the alarm that alerted the authorities, and the panic room. Jason had designed the basement to transform into an impenetrable safe-haven whose vault-like security measures could be triggered if necessary from the upstairs.

They had decided that it was best to contact the police only if there was an emergency, that way less had to be explained, and Han could keep his anonymity. The cameras' viewpoints could be seen on any screen in the house. The cave went into lockdown mode by pulling down on a handle that was housed inside of Milly's spice cabinet.

"What does this threat look like Jason?" Stella suddenly demanded.

"A woman, a type of private investigator. I've been treating her husband."

"How does she know about Han?"

"I did a trade, treatment for help getting to know my son. I know it was stupid, but I wanted to gather more information, to win Han over for this custody thing. You know, be the father he wants."

"Oh my God Jason! This woman interviewed for the coaching job. She was in our house! I don't know who's crazier, you with your hair brained schemes, or me for not calling the cops right now."

Han was spending an awfully long time down there, and everyone was wishing he'd come up. They decided to give him thirty more minutes.

The TV went on and the three of them plopped onto the living room couch, weary from the whole reunion process.

———

The thrown helmet caused one of the attackers to skid, fall, then slide in a display of orange sparks. "Ahhhhhhhh!" he screamed in agony as his hip collided with concrete.

"Back on the bike, back on the bike!" Aeson ordered.

Han hugged around Aeson's waist and looked back to see the bikes being confronted by a pair of SAM dogs. They were being asked to show I.D. and told that medical help was on its way. Aeson eased the bike into starting and tried to roll away as coolly as possible.

"You O.K. buddy?" Aeson asked Han while looking in his mirror for any more trouble.

"Yeah, are you cool Han?" continued Steven.

"He can't hear you Steven, he kinda lost his helmet," Aeson explained.

"I would forget the Peace Monument for now Aeson," Steven said, "you got a fight tonight and Han needs to go home and chill."

"We're on the same wavelength Steven," Aeson reported as he turned down the much less guarded exit out from Queens and back onto the interstate.

"Not to mention those Secular Army cops wondering where that helmet came from," Steven added.

"Nice move on Han's part," Aeson continued, trying to ease his own nerves with conversation. After barely getting away from an organized gang of chain swinging mad men while ignoring the warnings about violent fundamentalists, even a hardened fighter like Aeson began to shake.

"I did lose my helmet," Han realized out loud, at the same time closing his eyes and enjoying the air on his face. Every day should be for simple enjoyments, he thought. Just then a revving sound began to build behind him. As Han looked back he realized one of the bikers had returned, and just secured a tight grip onto the back of his jacket! Aeson felt the bike become much lighter and could hardly believe the image in his mirror of a man to his left grabbing Han and swinging him onto the back of his motorcycle. The terror of being passed between moving motorcycles left Han unaware, he hadn't even noticed the syringe that dangled from the back of his neck.

They dipped down into a short tunnel, and when they emerged Aeson could see the kidnapper, minus Han.

"Shit!" Aeson screamed.

"Don't worry, I'm still connected to his camera," Steven said. "He jumped off and grabbed the overhang. He's running on all fours straight towards the upper deck of the subway stop."

"Yes! Nice work Steven, let's just pick him up now and get home."

"Aeson! Han just jumped onto the top of the N-Train! He's heading to Times Square!"

———

The afternoon news was on, but paying attention to it seemed like just another distraction from the truth.

"Have you thought about the custody agreement?" Jason asked while lowering the volume on the television.

"I'm leaving it up to him. That was the original plan," Stella snapped, feeling the anger again of being abandoned and the confusion of still not being sure what Han's father was really up to.

"These are the facts Stella. The people who came that night and took me away want the secret to successful interspecies hybridization. I have convinced them after all these years of working on their shadow experiments that only I can unlock this mystery."

"By studying our son!"

"By gathering data based on his healthy experiences in a safe environment," Jason responded, causing Stella to look at him with the same Spartan demeanor she held when they took him away. "Believe me when I say that the conditions will be better than what their labs could provide. And everything will be above board and legal. They like when things are legal."

"What about going public? If everyone knows Han, and sees him for the person he is, he'll be safe."

"I might be willing to take that risk, but is that really our decision?"

Stella paused, and pondered the fates that may have cursed her son.

"And what about your old group, the original ones? I know you're still in touch in with them. How are they involved?"

Jason picked up the controller and increased the volume. "Jason! Jason I asked you a question."

Jason ignored Stella and began texting.

"Jason!" she shouted.

"Look at the TV Stella. It's Han, and he's climbing a building in Times Square."

———

Steven guided Aeson to the West Side Drive. He could jump on it just before getting on the George Washington. He was speeding and passing cars while trying to listen to Steven's directions, and then, suddenly, it was too late. His twelve year old protégé, nephew of his new fight manager and Aeson's complete and total responsibility when no one else is home, had ridden, and thankfully survived, on top of a speeding subway car, and was now climbing a building in one of the biggest tourist areas in the world.

"Aeson... Aeson! You missed the turn!"

"Left or right!"

"It was left, oh God, just take the first exit off the..."

"Aeson on hearing the direction and with barely a glance turned his bike, popped a wheelie, and drove screaming but with total focus over the embankment and onto the West Side Drive nearly fifteen feet below.

"Holy! Holy! Holy!"

"Whoooo! Let's get this kid!"

Luckily, or by the grace of some higher power, or by the aid of advanced motorcycle technology, Aeson's bike landed safely, avoiding all the thousands of tons of automobiles racing around him. "I knew MMA fighters had to be crazy," spoke Steven, in disbelief and shock about what had just happened.

"Nah, my dad and I used do a lot of motocross. So where is he now?"

"Hang on, holy shit, Aeson, he's on Eyewitness News!" Steven noted. The physically immobile boy felt as if his low rent quarters had become a war room and he wanted to open up windows to every angle he could find on the situation.

They turned down 42nd street and broke past the Port Authority station. Aeson was hit with the smells of roasting pretzels, puddles of urine, horse dung, and vehicles of every sort. Now this is New York.

"It's mini-King Kong!" someone yelled.

He was just four stories high like he was in Newark, only this was a lot different. If Aeson was overwhelmed by the hustle, bustle, noise and lights, what must Han have been going through? And what the hell was in that syringe that guy stuck in him?

"Poor thing. Look how it's dressed, must be an escaped illegal pet!"

The electric billboards all around relentlessly flashed images of smiling faces, steaming food, movie scenes, and sports highlights. As dusk began to fall over the city the digitized glitter only became more pronounced. Han's hands were still feeling the stress of clinging to the moving train for so long, and now all the distractions were making him want to scream.

"Hope it doesn't fall."

Perhaps coincidence, perhaps jinx, but at that moment crowds of people howled at once as the so-called ape in human clothing lost his footing and tumbled. His hands flailed and it looked as if at one point he caught hold of a ledge. Then he fell again and disappeared into the street watchers' blind spots.

"I see him. He hit the top of Madame Tussad's Wax museum!" notified Steven.

A camera crew was out in full force, having just finished shooting a story about street performers who claim to have super powers. There was a van with open doors and several of their crew were making an attempt to climb the museum's awning. A police officer had just arrived on the scene and was calling for back up.

"Aeson leave the bike but take your helmet with you. He's in the museum. He literally rolled in, and nobody even noticed him."

Steven could see from Han's clipped camera that he was inside and had stopped in front of the World Leaders' exhibit. He was simply staring at the diminutive Mahatma Ma Ghandi wax statue before something made him bolt. He ran on all fours. He blew past the feet of Elvis Presley, Michael Jordan, Neal Armstrong, and then Marilyn Monroe. He stopped in front of a blue skinned man who was clad in golden armor and held a bow; a quiver and arrows on his back. Han stared into the figure's transcendent eyes and began to get sleepy. He tried to speak, but only animal sounds came out. In his mind, probably from some humanities class memory, he had identified the image before him as Ram, the mightiest in the Hindu pantheon. The statue was big, and safe, so he crawled behind it and curled up.

Aeson entered and saw that the people inside were treating it as just another day in the metropolis. They may have heard that an ape like creature was climbing on a building, but nobody seemed to be impressed. "Ticket?" a heavily make-upped lady asked him.

The Wax Museum was packed with tourists who were being encouraged to take selfies. They were so into suspending disbelief you could have shouted Fire! and they would have thought it was part of the show.

"Find the *ANCIENT GODS* exhibit. I think he passed out there," reported Steven.

"You can get up little one," a generous confident voice told Han.

"What? Where am I? Who are you?"

"I am you, and you are… in New York City."

"How did I?"

"That does not matter. Your mother is worried. You must get home."

Han looked upon the form speaking to him so plainly and saw a creature that reminded him of the *Celestial Monkey* from a Kung-Fu movie he watched with his uncles.

"I, we, have many names, but Hanuman is my first. Whatever name we go by our duty is to serve what is good and help those who are helpless. That is what counts. Remember be who you really are, embrace your true self, share it when the time is right."

"Are you saying I should research my own experience?" Han asked Hanuman groggily causing the angelic visitation to take pause.

"Something like that," he answered.

"But I'm so tired, that guy injected me with something."

"Nothing can harm you, young Hanuman, when you embrace your true self." The vision imploded in a playful swirl of light tracers and Han no longer felt tired.

The figure who had floated before him was majestic and emanated trustworthiness. He left Han feeling less burdened and more energized, despite the challenges that he knew lay ahead. The primal urges to climb and scream, and escape into an animal ecstasy had not only receded but felt controllable. The beautiful monkey god who visited him disappeared back into whatever mystical or imaginative realm he came from.

As he shook off any residual effects of the tranquilizer he heard the voice of his coach. "Han, dude. Thank God we found you. Put this helmet on. Walk tall and move slow. We're getting out of here."

Chapter 14
THE SAME FEAR

"He's not here! I've checked already!" yelled Grandpa from the gym. As soon as Vincent opened the door the voices of strain and exercise ceased. Han had pulled one over on the old man by hooking up the audio recording of his last three workouts to the surround sound. "Smart kid," he murmured to himself.

"We checked everywhere upstairs and Aeson's new motorbike is gone," Grandma let him know.

"Was that really our Han on the news climbing a building?"

"That's what it looks like Vincent," answered Milly with worry in her voice.

Stella shot up and was the first one at the front door when they heard the motorcycle pull up.

Han wore Aeson's helmet which was way too big for him. His clothes were scuffed and scraped. Aeson wore the child's size skateboarding headgear he had bought from a cart while waiting at a red light. White skulls were emblazoned all over its black surface.

"We saw you on the news Han! Are you OK? What were you doing out? Do you need your treatment? Aeson does he need his treatment?"

"He's... good to go Mrs. Zucharino. He shifted and I thought he would need it, but he turned it around."

"What do you mean? He controlled the primal regression without the treatment?" a voice from the living room asked.

"Who's that?" Han stepped forward and asked.

"Honey, you're alright," Stella said as she took hold of the helmet and gently lifted it off.

"Who is that in there mom?"

"It's, it's your father."

———

They both pulled his bed out from beneath the grow lights and water misters. "I will stand and prepare," Majstro stated, signaling Katie to move next to him and shoulder some of his weight.

Senga watched knowingly from the doorway. He slid back into the other room as Majstro rose up.

The green man was made of muscle and chlorophyll. He could breath oxygen as well as photosynthesize. Like Han, he was one of a kind. As a regular man Majstro could be perfectly still in a sniper's crouch for record breaking lengths of time. Badgley's files showed that since his hybridization the duration he could wait without moving was undetermined. Majstro had become a near perfect assassin.

"Can I get you anything?" Katie asked him. She was bubbling with excitement despite her injuries but doing her best to not disturb the sanctity of the moment.

"Pants Katie. I'm not wearing any pants."

"Of course, oh my gosh, pants," she stammered out before buzzing past Senga towards her husband's wardrobe.

Majstro stood tall and widened his chest. He inhaled deeply, closed his eyes, and balled his fists. He began to whisper to himself in Japanese as he breathed out. Senga nodded slowly in approval as he watched from within the shadows.

"I have khakis, Carharts, and blue jeans. Which do you..." Katie was silenced by the patient's newest efforts. His features had begun to move and remold themselves. His nose became more shapely, ears were appearing, and grass-like shoots began to rise from his head, forming a thick covering of green hair.

"Hand me the pigment Katie." His wife dropped the clothes on the bed and rifled through more syringes, test tubes, and petri dishes. "Got it. Epidermal-Caucasian?"

"Hand it to me."

Majstro inserted the veterinary sized needle where the carotid artery is usually housed, and pushed. He began to take on the appearance of a square jawed white man in his thirties. After he pulled the needle out he walked into the other room with a dancer's poise and a predator's stealth.

Katie watched from the shadows this time, as Majstro and Mr. Senga kneeled before each other in the dark. Their hands began to form different interlocking patterns, and they whispered incantations. Katie knew they were finished when Majstro uttered a word she understood; "Tonight."

———

Han walked passed Stella, Milly, and Vincent, and towards the strange man who stood in his living room. The person turned his head quickly to hide his features, then pulled on his hood.

"Is it really you Dad?"

He turned slowly but hung his head, keeping his face hidden. "Yes, Han, it's me, your father, Dr. Jason Badg..."

"My dad?"

"Your dad, Han," he said as he knelt down. He placed his hands on his son's shoulders, and looked straight into his eyes. "You must hate me, and for good reason. I have so much to tell you, and teach you, if you want."

Han took a step back and gently shrugged off the hands.

"From what I heard, it sounds like you had a primal regression. Is this true?"

"I guess so," Han answered obstinately as he stared at the hideous man who helped give birth to him.

"You seem fine now. How did you return to equilibrium without the treatment?"

He shrugged again, trying to make light of this accomplishment and answered, "I think I fell asleep. I had a dream or something."

"Did the dream help you control it Han?" Jason asked with signs of being pleased appearing on his textured face.

"I guess so."

"One more question son, then I'll stop. Did anyone follow you?"

"No."

"Yo Han! Help yuz uncles carry this stuff in!" Salvatore yelled from the driveway.

Jason put his head down and typed in another text message.

Barely noting Sal's uproarious entrance Aeson turned towards Stella and apologized, "I'm sorry, I'm really sorry."

"Because you broke your agreement or because you got caught?" she asked. "For now the important thing is he's safe. We'll talk about how reckless you two were later."

"Hey! Somebody help me and Al!" Sal shouted from sweat coated jowls. He held a tan rolled up mat that was heavy enough to make him perspire as he squeezed through the doorway. "It's for tonight. Latest thing. We put these up in the gym, and voila, we got a new VIP room. This way Aeson and Han won't bump into each other anymore."

Sal pushed passed his sister and the fighter, saw that there was tension, and looked for what was going on in the living room.

"Hello Salvatore," spoke Badgley who was hoodless and utterly shocking to Sal.

Sal let the mat drop with a heavy thud, "Hi you doing Jay. Long time no see."

"Long time Sal."

"Well, we'll have a good audience for the fight tonight," was Sal's nonchalant response.

Stella irritably walked out of the room saying, "Really Sal, that's all you can think of right now? Ya damn gambling and the fights."

Sal shrugged his shoulders and asked with his own brand of sincerity, "What'd I say?" He was looking forward to having a cocktail on the ride back from Brooklyn, now he was in need of one.

Al came next bearing the same burden, "There's ten more of these in the car!"

"There's no fight tonight Sal. I'm sorry," spoke Aeson regretfully.

"Jason! Holy cannoli!" blurted Al.

"What do you mean no fight tonight guy?" Sal questioned Aeson.

Han jumped on top of one of the living room chairs, "It was my fault. I convinced Aeson. You all hired him to train me right? To prepare me for what comes next? You don't know what it's like to be cooped up all day, to only meet people on-line, to be me."

A single tear ran down Han's face and fell onto his mother's heart, breaking it in a million pieces. From the doorway Stella spoke, "You're right Han, I'm sorry baby, none of us know what it's like to be you."

Stella let the welling of water in her own eyes flow. She watched as her ex-husband took hold of her son's hand. Han remained defiant on top of the chair, but listened to what his father had to say. "It seems like some facts need to be discussed now, everything else, perhaps... in the morning, once everyone's emotions have settled," Jason said addressing the whole family. In Stella's opinion he was acting as if he was the head of the house and suddenly she had to repress a new emotion that was rising in her. Jason looked at his phone again and said, "Please leave the gate open, they're here."

Stella erupted, "Who! Who is here Jason!"

The vehicle that silently pulled into the Zucharino's driveway looked more like a Japanese automated race car then a police vehicle. Two SAMs, one male, one female, approached the house. The woman held Han's second damaged helmet in her hands.

"Saluton," they both said, and waited to be invited in.

Sal's eyes looked them over. He ran his fingers through his hair and dried his hands on his shirt. They both wore blue armored body suits, form fitting and flexible. Their perfect postures and black sunglasses gave them the demeanor of robots. Sal's gaze settled on the woman before he returned the greeting his own way, "Salut! How you doin?"

Jason intervened. "Saluton. Thank you for coming so quickly." The two special police bowed politely. Stella noticed that they held their heads down lower and longer in order to greet Jason. Stella rolled her eyes. Jason explained, "Han, these are Secular Army Marshalls."

"I know who they are," Had said timidly. "Thanks for returning my helmet," he told the woman and shyly smiled.

Unlike the hordes of people who seemed shocked and even scared of him in Times Square this woman made nothing of his extraordinary appearance. Instead she approached him and placed a gloved hand on his cheek.

"We are here to help," she said as she took off her glasses and gazed at Han softly. "Did someone try to hurt you today Han?"

Han stepped off the chair and let his heart rate slow, "I think some guys were trying to kidnap me."

"Oh my God!" cried Stella as she put her face in her hands.

For once Sal and Al waited without talking. Vincent and Milly held each other's hands.

The tall male SAM retrieved a digital sketch pad from his belt and prepared to interview the witnesses.

"I have an idea of who's behind this, and I'm not going to let anything bad happen to you," Jason iterated.

———

Majstro drove the RV. He wanted to be close to the house but he needed to retrace Katie's work first. Katie swallowed nervously, "It's right here, just turn in and pull under these trees."

He stepped out of the vehicle, closed the door, and became motionless. Katie was scared for a moment that the treatment had worn off. It was so peculiar, seeing him with his old skin tone. Unless you touched him, no one would be able to tell the difference. He lowered into a crouch and began to analyze the ground. Katie breathed in nervously. He walked over to where Dan Portman's tent had been then began to look towards the cliffs.

Majstro stared down below at the unforgiving rocks and shook his head with disappointment. Dan Portman's body had been visited at night by scavengers. His mouth, finally exposed by a jagged tear, appeared to be smiling up with a big lipless white toothed grin. "Katie," he called out, "Katie!" Before she could even make eye contact he hit her with the back of his hand, hard enough to draw blood. She hung her head.

Majstro continued his tracking and resumed his crouch. He didn't track like he was taught to in sniper school anymore, he had graduated to a more efficient technique. The plants told him what had passed in a language that most mammals could not comprehend. "They're all together! We must strike tonight!"

Katie picked her head up slowly and wore a thin smile on her glistening red mouth. She licked her lips and her eyes opened with a new brightness.

———

Jason, the two marshals, and Stella, returned to the spot in the woods where Jason had been led by his enhanced crow. "This is it, I'm sure of it."

The male spoke into his collar phone. The female SAM looked over the cliff as directed by Dr. Badgley. She was without emotion. They tracked the area and spoke quietly to Jason. Stella went to the cliff's edge when they were talking, but saw only rocks, water, and scraggly trees. There were no tire tracks. Everything had been wiped clean.

———

When Han heard them return he made sure to be the one to open the door. When he saw both his mother and father standing together his old childhood wish list came back to him, and a complete family was on the top. "What would you like to do tonight Han? It seems we're all together, how should we spend our time?" his father asked him.

"Wait, I'm not in trouble?"

"Nobody said that mister," Stella corrected.

"Your mother and I have discussed this matter..." Jason said making Stella fight the urge to roll her eyes and scream, "and we've decided that consequences can be met out tomorrow. You have been through a lot, and tonight... tonight is for our family."

Han looked up at his father and noticed how strange it was for such a careful intelligent voice to come out of such sadly misshapen features. He gazed into the kitchen and saw his old grandparents, patient and steady, back at his teary mom, full of love and confusion, his uncles moving mats, sweaty and eager to play, and Aeson, the fighter, who put his job and probably his life on the line to help him.

Han answered his dad. "It is fight night."

———

I'm probably in major trouble, but not till tomorrow! R U still up for meeting in the bleachers?

Of course!

"Yes!" Han said to himself as he read Kat's reply. Aeson was already warming up in the portable VIP room while cooking and other activities were taking place upstairs. "Bling! Bling!" Holy cannoli, who else could possibly show up today wondered Han. The driveway gate buzzer usually gave time for the family to check the video before letting anyone in. Al and Sal must have left it open when they were unloading their cargo.

"I'll get it!" Han shouted but remembered that he wasn't usually allowed to answer the door. When he got up the stairs he squatted and peaked from behind the banister. Stella was talking with a woman. Han thought of those guys in Queens who were after him. He had always suspected that his father was involved with shady characters. Could this be the work of some grim associate of his dad's, paparazzi who tracked them from Times Square, or some crazed fundamentalist who wanted to win a place for himself in heaven by slaying an abomination?

He crept up an inch closer, and who he set his eyes on completely took him by surprise. The young woman who stood at the door was dressed in denim, had a duffle bag over her shoulder, and could not hide her rustic beauty beneath a beat up ball cap.

"Hi Mrs. Zucharino. I decided to take you up on your offer."

It was none other than Aeson's girlfriend, Lenora.

———

Majstro and Katie had sat quietly in the darkness of the RV, listening to the sounds the doctor, his ex-wife, and two Secular Army Marshalls made as they looked for evidence.

Katie's mania to save her husband at all costs made her sloppy, and she was sure they were going to have to find other digs to launch their assault on the Zucharinos. She was amazed when Majstro had told her to start cleaning up the tracks. Katie watched in awe as Majstro closed his eyes and seemingly commanded the plant kingdom to grow around the vehicle! Within the span of an hour the Chinook had become a part of the New Jersey forest. So thick was the vegetation that Katie wondered just how they would get in and out. Majstro had considered mobility in his subterfuge so he molded the plant life so that the door could invisibly open and shut.

"Is the suit finished yet?" Majstro inquired.

"Still warm," she answered, and handed him the soft black material.

———

"He's downstairs sweetie," Stella let Lenora know.

"Well then I'll go down there and give him a big old hug if you don't mind," Lenora said. Her cowgirl mannerisms endeared her to Stella instantly.

"Women are bad luck before a fight," Vincent opened his eyes from his chair to say.

"It might be better to surprise him," Stella added just before Han broke in.

"After he wins!"

"Who was that?" Lenora asked, still curious about the special student her boyfriend had been working with.

"That was my son, Han," Stella heard herself say while wondering how to deal with the situation. The protocol had always been secrecy, but ever since they posted that job ad things had changed. "He might be a little shy, I'll ask him what he wants to do."

She's giving me an option Han pondered. It's going to be up to me. Before his mom could find him he emerged.

"Hi, I'm Han, you're my coach's girlfriend."

Maybe it was the sensitivity she acquired from working with horses, and all the equine therapy clients who visited her ranch, but she didn't bat so much as an eyelash.

"I sure am. Name's Lenora, pleasure to meet Aeson's favorite student!"

Their hands met and Han felt his mouth stretch into a big happy grin.

Al, Stella, Milly, and Lenora began to cook up a storm. Dr. Badgley remained reclusive, cloistering himself in Grandma's sewing room, persistently pecking away at the keyboard of his laptop. Han and Vincent went downstairs to help finish Aeson's warm up.

"Remember what the late great Cus D' Amato said kid," offered Grandpa, "*Heroes and cowards feel exactly the same fear. Heroes just react to it differently.*"

"I'll remember that Vincent," Aeson let Grandpa know.

"Let's hit mitts before you go in," Vincent said as he clapped the fighter on the shoulder.

"That really is good advice Grandpa," Han noted.

Aeson smiled and winked at Han while lightly boxing the air. "It works for getting dates too ya know."

Chapter 15
REMATCH

Valhalla was like one giant party, and Odin was filling guests' chalices to the brim. There were a lot of new avatars milling around, but Han was looking for one in particular.

"You like that? Designed it myself," Steven, aka Hephaestos told Han as he sipped the red digital liquid.

"Feels like my VIP suit is alive. Kinda tickles," Han told him.

"I'll keep working on it. Care for a nip of this, big man?" Hephaestos asked Aeson.

"Maybe after the fight. How's it taste?"

"No taste yet, more of a sensation, but that's just from what my guinea pigs tell me anyway. I don't really have a mouth, so…"

"So!" Han said jumping in, "Do you guys know what *Valhalla* actually means?"

"Tell us lad," a towering voice spoke, "I didn't know you were so well informed as to the meaning of my port room's name."

"Hall of the Slain!" was Han's energetic reply.

"Someone's excited about Norse mythology," commented Hephaestos sarcastically.

"Excited about mythology, or about a girl?" Aeson questioned rhetorically.

"Alright guy!" said Odin as he tried to give Han a high-five. When the Monkey King denied him the hand to hand contact he corrected himself, "I mean, good work wooing a maiden lad."

"Why did you choose *Hall of the Slain* for your port, why not, I don't know, something more modern?" asked Aeson.

"When we don the VIP skins our old selves are slain temporarily, so that our new ones can live," explained Odin.

"Very philosophical chief," replied Hephaestos to Odin's explanation, "now what's with all the new people?"

"In honor of Aeson The Fighter of course! I have taken it upon myself to promote."

"Thanks Odin," said Aeson sincerely. "I hope I make you guys proud. Now, I don't see any clocks in here. Anybody know what time it is?"

"Time to get beat, punk!" came a shout that was accompanied by a slap to the back of Aeson's head. The fighter felt the surprising sting and turned around enraged. The culprit was none other than his opponent The Guido Ritigliotti, and from the looks of him he either upgraded or he'd been lifting some serious weights. "That's right tough guy. You're still seeing straight. Ya ain't dreaming!" His neck alone looked as if it had packed on several inches of new muscle on each side. The Guido's arms were like boulders and his chest had pumped up to a cartoonish and massive size. Engorged veins rippled not only through his physique but created lay lines across his face and clean shaven head. His hands, feet, and head were the only parts that hadn't seemed to magnify in size.

"Yeah, what we're seeing is steroids, combined with growth hormones, combined with whatever else you bought from the black market to try to get the edge," said Hephaestos as he floated between the two who were about to brawl.

"Hey, it's the VIP freak. Remember, only thing you can't use is an avatar, and all this," he said as he directed attention to his physique, "this is all me baby!"

"Guido," said Odin, "the only reason I give you port access is because I respect your efforts on the battlefield and I want to support the Ultimate Underground."

"Yeah right! You're gonna make more coin tonight than me or this Colorado sissy. You love it that I'm in here!"

"Well your surly entrance is a good segway I suppose." Odin then raised his chalice high and gathered everyone's attention. Han saw a myriad of eccentric characters; some with wings, others with capes, horned creatures with cloven feet, handsome men in tuxedos, beautiful women in gowns, werewolves, knights, so many identities lifted from the pages of books and copied from popular movies. But where was the Hindu goddess Katya, Han wondered. Golden shields had been added to the room's wall décor and glistened onto the strange and wondrous faces. Odin continued as everyone gathered around the great table. "Ladies! Gentlemen! Heroes, villains, secret agents, and alien life forms, tonight is Fight Night! Let us enjoy a courageous battle!" The guests began to tap their chalices against the digital surface. "And... remember to see me if you have forgotten to place your bets."

"They have to expand their bleachers, this is the most people I've ever seen in here," noted Hephaestos as they searched for good seats.

"Aw c'mon statue-guy it just makes it more cozy," someone told them through the congestion. She stood up and opened all her arms to receive Han in a big hug. She was blue, and fierce, and in Han's eyes super cute.

"Katya!"

"Monkey King!"

"Katya, this is the guy I wanted you to meet."

"Name's Hephaestos, nice skulls," he said, commenting on the fist sized skinless craniums that now decorated her belt.

"Thanks, just added them today."

The two shook hands. Hephaestos' eyes began to analyze the coding of the skulls out of curiosity.

"Well I'd like you to meet someone too Han. This is Michael," Katya announced as a tall man with movie star looks rose from his seat. Han swallowed hard, and a weight began to drop on his heart. "He's my father! I finally convinced him!"

"Nice to meet you... sir," said Han shyly.

"And you are?" Majstro asked paternally, not wearing an avatar, but utilizing the father idea instead.

"I'm…"

"He's the Monkey King, Michael, protector of the weak, and guardian of the Tunnel," said Hephaestos.

"Pleasure to meet you Monkey King. This is quite a world you kids hang out in."

"Yeah, I love it."

The lighting over the bleachers began to dim, and a single spotlight gradually grew brighter in the center of the caged combat area. The announcer, whom Han had nicknamed The Shark, started to materialize before them. Everyone went quiet.

"Last time they clashed ladies and gentlemen we had a remarkable upset. The Guido was dethroned by a newbie!" The spotlight moved off The Shark and illuminated the monstrous Guido. The crowd cheered, some booed, and the sky above the cage began to glisten. Fans were signing in from all over the globe. With a wave of his hand the announcer guided the spotlight across the cage and onto Aeson. "But he is newbie no more!" The cheering multiplied and Han almost covered his ears. Aeson looked literally half his opponent's size as he lightly moved his feet and shook residual tension from his shoulders.

They touched gloves and Aeson could feel, even from just this tap, a strength in his opponent that could have knocked a man down in the outside world. "Ding!" The round began and they both came out charging. Aeson had speed on his side. His boxer's foot work and head movement helped to keep him away from Guido's bombing strikes. Guido punched the cage and Aeson could feel the very mat underneath him vibrate. The Fighter landed punch-kick combinations to his opponent's head and legs. The gargantuan wasn't fazed. Aeson kept moving and hitting but nothing could hurt this guy. The crowd began to boo. With ten seconds left in the first round Aeson felt distracted. His eyes wandered to the ticket audience and he felt revulsion at the high-end fans who were screaming to see damage. As he turned his head back to face Guido he was hit, hard. The VIP was supposed to be safe because of its virtual element, but Guido had changed the variables. For the first time in the virtual world Aeson felt real pain. His nose crunched underneath the force. In the padded room the suit compacted against his face so hard he could have sworn he heard it crack. The round was over and Aeson was breathing through his mouth. In his experience this was never a good sign.

"You got this coach! Next round is yours!" Han hollered.

"You sure about that Han? This other guy looks crazy strong," commented Katya.

"You'll see," was all Han could muster, he was so nervous for his mentor.

Katya took hold of his hand and said, "OK, if you say so."

Han didn't know whether to look at her or into the arena. He had never held hands with a girl before.

"Ding!" sounded for round 2 and Han unconsciously stood up and cheered with both his arms in the air, unknowingly breaking his grip with Katya. As he sat back down he neurotically worried that she may have felt slighted. He put his hand in hers again only to realize it was one of her extra appendages, she didn't feel it but she did notice his attempt. She smiled and he decided that tonight was the night. He was going to ask her out. Why should he be scared? After all he had learned Monkey Kung Fu in Newark, and escaped a kidnapping attempt in Queens. The SAMs as well as Lenora weren't freaked out by his appearance, and he was banking on the idea that Kat wouldn't be either.

Aeson wasn't sure if he broke even on the first round, but he certainly hadn't won. Round Two had to be a victory. Having to breathe through his mouth made him realize that he had broken his nose and that upset The Fighter greatly. No one ever broke his nose in the physical world. Han almost got kidnapped, and he was probably going to get fired from his coaching job. Lenora was most likely still upset with him over that rich woman's surprise kiss from the last fight. And he still had a lot of debt he owed the Colorado Fight Commission. He had learned to control his rage better than he ever had before in the last few weeks, but now he decided to call upon it. How else could he topple an enhanced behemoth?

They both charged, and as soon as they made contact Aeson had wished he hadn't. He got in a close quarter elbow and a driving knee but he should have kept his distance. The Guido dug his hands into his rib cage and wrapped them around his body. Usually in this situation Aeson would drop his center of gravity, make space, and use it as an opportunity to tee off on his enemy; not this time. Before he knew it he was in the air and his back felt like it was breaking. My God he thought, he broke my nose in the virtual world, what's going to happen to my spine? Suddenly for the first time in his fight career he thought he might tap out but then had the eerie thought that the ref might not stop it if his surrender wasn't complete and dramatic. Thousands, maybe millions of people were watching. He summoned every ounce of strength to straighten, and reverse the bend that was happening to his back. Guido only squeezed harder and laughed like a villainous chiropractor. "This is my world twerp!" he heard from his destroyer.

"Ahhhhh!" Aeson screamed as the pain became unbearable, he could resist no more. The homeless Kung-Fu master's flowing form came into his consciousness, and he remembered her drunken style. Every time she appeared off balance she was actually putting herself into a position of strength. Where was his strength? His spine bent further and he found himself staring into the glistening world above him.

"Tap punk! Tap! If I kill you it's on you!"

Aeson's head continued to tilt backwards and he began to bend into the crushing force instead of fighting it. The unorthodox movement could have ended him, but before Guido could unleash a final killing crush Aeson realized he had created enough space to lift his legs and wrap them around the Guido's waist. As soon as his ankles crossed his spine was able to return to a healthier position. His head flowed to attention and Guido's strength couldn't work as effectively against him.

"You're a dead man," came out of Guido's maw but was muffled by Aeson's torso against his face. It was time to make this position work for him. If he jumped off it might give Guido a chance to hit him in the nose again so he began to deliver short punches to his opponent's ears, irritating the chemically enhanced combatant to no end. Guido began to run.

Slam! The whole cage reverberated as the muscle bound maniac drove the fighter into the fence. The fans cheered; all booing ceased.

"Keep fighting Aeson!" Han yelled. As if he heard his student's words of encouragement, Aeson began to rally. Instead of dropping down and letting Guido get a better position Aeson continued to climb. He kept his ankles crossed but worked his way up Guido's frame with micro movements. Before he knew it his knees were in his opponent's arm pits, and the Guido did not like that. Even more irritating were the elbows Aeson began reigning down on top of his skull.

Aeson became even more tactical, calculating, and realized quickly that rage was not going to win this one. He hammered his crown and when he buried his head to avoid the blows that were probably more humiliating than painful Aeson would move back to boxing his ears. Guido screamed in frustration but there were two more minutes left on the round. This is where Guido made a fatal mistake.

Ritigliotti decided to press his hand on the back of Aeson's knee and simply continue to lift. He would pry one leg off at a time and leave The Fighter without his closed guard. He should have pushed on both legs at once though, because as soon as Aeson felt upward pressure he went with it and let his leg lift. Instead of falling off he swung it up and over Guido's neck. Re-crossing his ankles and securing a position on his arm, head, and neck. Aeson began to squeeze. The only problem was he felt like he was squeezing against concrete. Guido began to backpedal and Aeson knew he was going to try and slam him despite the strangulation hold. As he pulled away from the fence Aeson moved again. He used the bald head in front of him as a handle for both his hands and swung himself around so now he had the same triangle choke on Guido only from behind. He heard the marauder gag. Guido continued to run backwards and slammed Aeson into the fence again, but he wouldn't budge. He constricted with his thighs, his abs, and now his arms and upper body. With one minute left the Guido took a knee. Aeson relentlessly crushed taking big slow breaths in order to maximize his efforts. With ten seconds on the clock The Guido didn't tap out, he passed out, and his hulking body collapsed in a heap of super charged muscle.

The Ultimate Underground roared with excitement as did the whole of the Zucharino residence. They had watched the fight from the living room couch and even the scientifically minded Badgley had found himself caught up in the energy. "Good job!" he exclaimed.

"Good job, he just beat a giant Doc!" said Grandpa Vincent.

"Indeed he did," replied Jason.

Lenora sat in between Stella and Milly and realized she had been holding hands with them for the whole of the tenuous second round. "He did it honey," said Stella, "your Aeson is quite the fighter."

They watched as the announcer returned to raise The Fighter's hand. As was customary following such a dramatic victory he handed Aeson the mic.

"I'd like to thank my opponent, he's the first guy to break my nose." Guido managed a slight smile and gave Aeson a thumbs up, which the Fighter returned. "I'd like to thank Grandpa Vincent for his wise advice, Sal and Al for getting me hooked up with the UU, Stella and Milly for supporting me even when I don't deserve it, and Han, my single and absolute best student. You've definitely taught me more than I've taught you." Aeson looked towards the bleachers and waved triggering all occupiers of free seats to go bananas with shouts of appreciation. "But... there's someone else..." The crowd began to whisper, then went silent. "My girlfriend, my true love, Lenora back in Colorado I hope you're watching. Cuz I want you to know that fighting means nothing to me without you and what I'm about to do scares me more than The Guido." The audience seemed to gasp in unison. "Lenora, will you marry me?"

Lenora's eyes felt misty and her heart began to flutter. She knew in that moment there was only one answer.

The Shark took the mic back saying, "Is this guy great or what? Aeson The Fighter Cadmus, I hope we see a lot more of you in the Ultimate Underground."

Sal sipped on a fresh cocktail and said, "You better believe it baby."

Everyone began milling around again. Some wanted to keep the good energy alive in *Valhalla* or other favorite rooms. Hepahaestos asked Han if he could talk privately for a second. Han excused himself and they both moved away from the crowd. "What's up Steven? I mean Hephaestos."

"Let's say I'm Steven right now, your friend."

"Okay."

"I can't keep this in Han, it's about your Katya."

"Yeah?"

"I can't help but look at code, you know me dude, and your friend, who claims she's our age, well she isn't."

"What? What do you mean, is she already a teenager or something. That would still be cool I guess."

"No man, she's like thirty, at least."

Han's mind and body filled with foreign emotions. He had never been betrayed before. This couldn't be happening, unless she...

"No way Steven."

"Han, I'm not making this stuff up, and while I'm at it I got to tell you. Odin, he's..."

"My uncle, I know. I just let him think I don't know. He's just looking out for me. My uncles gave me the VIP room and they just want me safe, out of the *Tunnel* you know."

"OK, well that makes me feel a little better, but not about Katya. Dude, why would she be doing this?"

"She's not, and, and, I'll prove it."

The two were still in their seats when Han came back; "Katya, could I talk to you for a second?"

Taken off guard Katya looked at her father for direction. He nodded his head in approval.

They looked for a quiet place but found themselves right near the red carpet entrance of the UU. "What's up Monkey King?"

"Katya, Kat, are you, are you who you say you are?"

"What! Of course. Does your friend think otherwise, should I talk to him?"

Han noticed her four hands tighten into fists. "No, no, I just wanted to hear it from you."

"Okay then, can we go back now, my father's waiting."

"Just, one more thing. If you don't mind. The red carpet is an avatar remover. Can you step in with me, just for a second, so I can tell Hephaestos to chill out?"

Katie Carouch knew she had to think fast but for the life of her couldn't come up with a solution. What will Majstro say? "I don't know, my dad's here and all maybe…"

A mass of people who spotted their new MMA hero Aeson the Fighter Cadmus saved Han the trouble of pressing her. Within seconds of seeing Aeson on the red carpet people began to push through to get closer to him. Katya and Han were thrown into the mallei and found themselves standing atop a blood red programmed-to-feel-plush material.

"Oh my God. You really are a monkey!" was the last thing Han heard before the same blonde woman who had come to his house for the coaching interview shot up and blipped out of the VIP world.

Chapter 16
INHERITANCE

Everyone was celebrating upstairs when the doorbell rang, "Bling!"

Could we have left the gate open again Stella wondered. She looked through the peephole and heard a voice say, "Secular Army, may I come in?" Even though it was evening she was still in her dark glasses. Probably high-tech night vision gear or something Stella thought.

"Hi again," Stella said as she answered the door. This SAM had blonde hair tucked underneath a thick head band. It wasn't typical, so before the SAM could say anymore Stella poked her head out and looked at the driveway gate. It was still closed. "What the...?" Fear shot like ice through her rib cage and seemed to stop her heart for a moment. She stepped back to close the door but the woman not only pushed her way through she swept Stella's foot and punched her once in the liver area, dropping the utterly unprepared woman instantly.

"Badgley!" screamed Katie Carouche as she threw her sunglasses to the floor. The man who walked in behind her was so pale and stoic he looked like death itself thought Milly.

"Salvatore!" screamed Grandma.

"Pull the switch Ma! Lock the panic room!" Sal dropped his drink and shouted. Uncle Sal moved in as quickly as he could to run interference between the door and the kitchen. Majstro, without even looking, chopped once to Sal's neck with an open hand. He too fell instantly from the shock to his carotid artery.

Badgley heard the commotion and figured out quickly what was happening. He pressed his back against the wall and retrieved his phone. It was immobilized. The sinister couple had used Majstro's black apps to jam communications.

Han's father had coached Milly extensively on the protection protocol and hoped she'd act accordingly. The doctor grabbed his lap top and made a mad dash for the cave.

———

As soon as Katie disappeared from the red carpet Han realized what was happening. He kicked his VIP door open and shouted towards the gym, "Aeson! I think there's going to be trouble upstairs. The cave's going to lock down!"

In the middle of signing an autograph on the red carpet Aeson stood to attention. Was there a voice in his head? "Trouble upstairs!" he swore he heard again. A gust of air suddenly hit his sweat soaked suit and he remembered he was in the gym's portable VIP. He suddenly blipped out of the virtual world and realized the door had been pushed open.

Concern washed away any pride that came from his bout with Guido and he bolted for the door. As Aeson made his exit he could see Han in a blur dive rolling through the doorway that was fast being sealed by a heavy piece of metal. Without thinking he followed, jumped, and barely made it in before the panic room sealed itself with no way to open for twenty-four hours.

Clad in their form fitting VIP clothing and with only their faces revealed, they both ripped off their goggles and looked at each other.

"That lady! There is no Kat! This isn't a test!" Han blurted out.

"Stay here Han," Aeson told the kid as he climbed his way up.

Han watched as his coach flew up the stairs and kicked open the door between the kitchen and living room. Aeson had knocked into Han's father who had attempted to enter the panic room. A cacophony of terrible sounds poured down upon Han along with Badgley's laptop. Mom, Grandma, everyone was up there! He remembered Grandpa's words then, as well as the strange vision he had in the wax museum, and just went for it. "Yeeeeee!" he screamed, not as a primal regression, but as a battle cry.

His father was gone by the time Han made it out of the cave's staircase. Uncle Sal was on his hands and knees in the kitchen, with both his arms wrapped around one of the blonde woman's legs. The imposter lady was dragging him on her way towards Grandma who still had both hands on the panic lever within the cabinet. His mom was crawling towards him and desperately screamed, "Han! Get in the cave."

"Too late!" he shouted as he leapt with all his might towards the kitchen. It was no ordinary jump, rather the specific martial technique that Lulu had shown him, *Monkey Flies Into Sky*. It felt like he had become made of iron in mid-air. "Yeeeee!" he used his landing to launch *Attacking Iron Wall*, and Katie fell hard as the wind gushed from her lungs. She stood, even though Han's Kung-Fu technique must have done more damage to her already wounded body. This crazed woman was driven by adrenaline and fight madness. Katie's eyes had filled with blood because of the concussive force of Han's hybrid muscularity, but she kept coming. To the Zucharino clan she looked nothing short of demonic. Han turned for a second to see if his mother was OK. They met eyes and Han heard her scream "Duck Han! Duck!"

"Duck?" He looked down at Sal and he reiterated his mom's message in a tired plea, "Get down kid." Han acted and hit the deck only to see a throwing star being released from the woman's hand. It stuck deeply and with a thud in the wall behind him. He attacked again and this time he knew he had to knock her out. He leaped up and an explosion went off behind him. The four pointed weapon blew up three seconds after impact and its force seemed to propel him even harder towards the home invader. Han's right hand curled into a bent fist and his wrist bone made contact with Katie Carouche's jaw. Lights out.

Where was everyone else? The front door was open. They're outside!

Aeson, Han's dad, and Lenora, were all facing off with the imposter's so-called father. The tall man's pale complexion had begun to turn a vomit green, and as he entered a deep wide-kneed stance, Han realized he was a lot scarier than the woman.

Aeson moved up as Badgley dropped back. The scientist was intent on contacting help. Lenora was looking around for a weapon and had one hand up as if the off-green man was a berserk stallion. Han rolled into position next to Aeson. Their black VIP skins glistened in the moonlight.

Aeson attacked with a Thai push kick, but Majstro moved only a few inches out of the way. As the fighter's foot went by him Majstro intercepted his leg with a quick punch. The strike was to his sciatic nerve and Aeson's lower body went numb. He fell to his knees and Han knew he was going to strike him again, this time the blow might be lethal.

Han tried *Attacking Iron Wall* again but it had little effect besides leaving him vulnerable beneath the man's stance. Majstro chopped once downwards towards Han's neck, and even though it only grazed him the sting was painful. Han rolled but didn't want to leave Aeson exposed.

His coach was crawling and trying to stand when Majstro delivered a palm strike to his crown. Han watched as Aeson's body began to convulse in a seizure. "Aeson!" Lenora shouted as she hurled a brick towards the attacker. To her horror the evil man's hand shot up and caught it, as easily as catching a ball in a mitt.

"Badgley!" he commanded, "Surrender or watch your son die!" and with that the brick shot out of his hand and into Han's midsection. He doubled over in pain but knew he had to keep fighting. "You must understand. We are the same you and I. Your father must remove the shackles of dependence that he put on both of us!" he lectured Han. As Han stood he felt the man's hands upon him. His grip was industrial; a crushing, merciless force.

In the kitchen Stella and Vincent were attempting to bind Katie's hands behind her back. Before they could secure the knot her eyes opened and she screamed a banshee cry through froth and blood covered lips. She pushed backwards to kneeling and jumped to her feet. Easily breaking her unfinished bonds she grabbed a knife from the counter and began to swing. Grandpa, Grandma, and Stella picked up weapons of their own, a broom, a chair, and a cordless mixer. Vincent pushed at her like a lion tamer, Stella poked at her eyes with the broom disorienting her vision, and Milly used the hand mixer to fend off the blade.

"Badgley!" the off-green man screamed as he tightened his now secure hadaka-jime choke hold on Han. Han could see Lenora beneath him dragging Aeson to a safer location, and he spotted his father in the driveway attempting to make a phone call from the roof of Uncle Sal's car. "Drop the phone or the boy dies!" was the last thing Han heard before blacking out.

When he opened his eyes he realized he was free from the man's grasp, and his father's phone was at his feet. "Take it up the tree," he heard his father struggle to say, "It's dialing but needs to be out of their blocking range." The off-green man and Han's father were locked in each others' grasps. Han was relieved when he realized the man needed his father alive. "Now Han, climb!" Majstro rammed Badgley against the tree to block Han with both their bodies. They each had a hand on the other's throat and wrist. "Now!" his father commanded.

Han jumped onto the man's back and used his head as a footstall. He put the phone in his mouth and climbed faster than he had ever done before.

Katie had driven the three defenders backwards and they were now all bleeding from lacerations. She ran to the exit as soon as she could and the three injured family members pursued.

"Hello! Hello! This is Han Zucharino! My father is Jason Badgley! We need help!" Han desperately shouted into the screen, scaring a squirrel from its nest in a flurry of grey fur.

Badgley could see his bleeding ex-wife charging the knife wielding maniac. Han might have not gotten through to the SAMs, and if he did, would it be too late? Badgley knew he had to do something drastic. He concentrated on his cybernetic hand that held Majstro's throat and triggered an electric defense tazer to protrude from his wrist. A thin metal rod pushed out from where tendons normally would be. He stared into Majstro's crazed eyes as he sent 50, 60, then 70,000 volts into his neck!

Majstro stepped backwards in an attempt to break the doctor's grip, ripping them both away from the tree. Grandpa and Grandma had their backs to the two combatants as they faced Katie. Katie Carouche could see her husband's head buzzing with blue electricity and increased the propensity of her own attack. She slashed at Vincent's forearms and the chair fell.

Stella was jabbing at Majstro's neck as Katie prepared to run her through. Jason increased the voltage, and felt Majstro weaken. When he realized Stella was about to be impaled he used every ounce of strength from his own simian musculature and turned the assassin around, smashing the assassin's back against the tree, but still leaving Stella exposed. Majstro's eyes began to close and his body started to root itself. Badgley tried to break free from the plant/mammal hybrid he helped create but to no avail. The assassin's grip on his wrist had changed. His very fingers were now vines which wrapped the doctor's entire arm.

Jason feared the worst for Stella, but then he heard Han's cry, "Yeeee!" and looked up to see his son descending in mid-air. Han hit the ground right next to Stella and pushed her out of the way of the oncoming blade. Katie's relentless charge however was irreversible, and the knife, guided by the force of the madwoman's rage, stabbed deeply into Dr. Jason Badgley's lung. The blade pierced his heart, and his eyes too began to close.

The desperate and terribly wounded family descended on Katie. By the time they were done Lenora had hog-tied her with a garden hose. Everyone was panting and there was blood everywhere. The SAMs, whose vehicle had been disabled by the electromagnetic spike traps Katie had set for them, had ran from the street and had to climb over the security gate. Han had gotten through to them. For Han's father it was too late.

More Secular Marshals showed up along with a medical team. The new world cops were in a hurry to secure the area. They had their own ambulances, and after being pried away from the hardened roots that were once Majstro's fingers Dr. Badgley's body was taken away and disappeared in a whirr of lights and sirens. The green man was rooted to the ground below him so the SAMs had no choice, at least for the time being, to leave him where he stood. Carouche was taken away in a Secular Army police car.

Han had refused attention because everyone but he and Lenora were either unconscious or suffering from bad knife wounds.

———

The family checked themselves out of the private Queen's medical facility before just before dawn.

Everyone including the SAMs were horrified to see that Majstro's body was nowhere to be found.

An investigation was conducted and many interviews transpired. The marshals had offered therapeutic services but everyone refused. There was consensus within the Zucharino family that they needed time to process together and for now without outside help.

"Is that Dr. Badgley's laptop?" the soft spoken female SAM asked Han. He was cradling it in his arms and staring at the blank screen of the living room's television.

"Is it my dad's?" he snapped.

"Yes, is that your *dad's* Han?" she continued.

"It's mine!" he insisted as he squeezed it tighter. The SAM conceded, nodded her head, and walked away.

When the officers left, the family, bandaged, medicated, and traumatized, gathered near the big tree, and stared blankly at the site of the murder.

"Where is he?" asked Aeson.

"What was he?" questioned Lenora.

"He's a hybrid, like me, the first human-plant of his kind," answered Han. "He was a soldier who volunteered for enhancement. Majstro is his code name. He's, a private contractor now." Han said these things and looked around nervously, as if the off-green man were about to jump up from the earth and grab him.

"Han, honey, he's dead. This bad man is gone, Jason... your father, killed him."

"No. Plants go into a dormant state when burned or electrocuted. He was only sleeping."

The group had organically formed themselves into a circle of physically and emotionally exhausted people. They stared at Han in disbelief.

"Honey, Han," his mother asked, "how do you know all this?"

"Dad's lap top. It was easy to hack. Most of the passwords requested were stuff about me."

"Hey! Guys! What the heck happened?"

Everyone turned their heads at once to see Uncle Al, clad in his VIP suit, looking around at the siege's aftermath in utter confusion. His great belly, thin legs, and utter ignorance as to the horror that went down gave everyone permission to smile, even if it was just for a moment. The twelve hour time lock opened on the cave.

Aeson looked at Han for an answer, so he gave one. "Say hi to Odin, my uncle Al, keeper of the *Valhalla* porthole. In the VIP world nothing is as it seems."

————

The quiet funeral was a testament to Dr. Badgley's covert life. The event was attended by a few Secular Army dignitaries, several soft spoken scientists, and his nuclear family. Han wore his glasses but didn't bother covering up his identity. He was out he had decided, from now on.

The New Jersey house had been restored entirely and came complete with an alarm system that linked directly to Secular Army security stations. Three weeks after Jason Badgley was buried Han's mother introduced him to someone. "This is your father's attorney."

"I was your father's friend as well. We were in college together."

The man parted his hair to one side, wore glasses, and kept his brief-case at his feet.

"Are you here to tell me about my father?"

"No Mr. Zucahrino. I'm here to tell you about your father's will. You have inherited quite a bit. His house in New York state, multiple laboratories, both national and international, as well as all of his overseas holdings are now yours, despite what the Secular Army lawyers are claiming."

Han nodded his head stoically in acknowledgement, but when the attorney left he put his face in his hands and cried. The tears were for the man he wished he had known.

In his tree Han was satisfied that his family, Aeson and Lenora included, were beginning to get back to some semblance of equilibrium. He knew they were planning something for him so he made himself invisible for a time. He let them prepare, cook, and decorate, to their hearts' content; for they all had very generous hearts. Han sat with the squirrel, who was so comfortable with his presence that he had curled up in a ball at Han's feet. He retrieved the laptop from his bag and the soft grey creature remained.

Han had continued to memorize, transfer, and even delete the files that he had poured over since his father was buried. There was one though that he continued to remunerate over. He must have read and re-read it a hundred times. It was the last message his father had ever sent and it was to an anonymously encrypted recipient. He recommitted it to memory, highlighted it, and hit delete.

When he entered the house he did his best to not only feign surprise but to appear happy. There were thirteen candles on the kiwi covered cake and eight people present. Lenora helped Aeson hook Steven in to the party via his phone. The floating statue was a welcomed guest as he sat shimmering on the small screen. They sang Happy Birthday and celebrated the very special boy who had just become a teenager.

Lenora showed everyone her ring and Aeson pointed out the new shape of his nose. Han, even though he was the guest of honor, had a surprise of his own for everyone. His humanities project was finally complete and everyone was reinvigorated to see what he had come up with.

"Everyone has one. Don't be shy, just go and get changed and meet me downstairs," Han directed as he handed out freshly printed VIP suits.

They all stood in the gym's larger VIP space and froze as the lights went off. Suddenly everyone was transported to a new world that Han had designed.

"Welcome to Queens New York, before we allowed a conflict of ideologies to take it away," Han announced to his guests.

They toured mosques, synagogues, churches, and temples. They heard various languages and were welcomed into homes. They danced, sang, laughed and cried. Han's humanities project was a hit with his online teachers as well. He had gone above and beyond to analyze a real historical conflict, identify its causes, and offer a solution. Han proposed that the VIP could be a true vehicle for peace, one that the Monkey King vowed to protect.

That night the family slept with uplifted spirits and the hope of the better world that their very special thirteen-year-old had shown them. Han, who had been sleeping in the great tree decided to climb down. He wanted to feel the earth beneath his feet. He began to perform the Kung-Fu he had been taught and soon his body was loose and his thinking felt flexible. His father's last email was the focus of his meditation and he looked at it again, in his mind's eye as he jumped, kicked, rolled, and flipped. The words no longer scared or even perplexed him. Han embraced them and everything that had unfolded, even if his understanding was not yet complete. He smiled up at the stars, at the bridge, and the big city in the distance. He turned north towards upstate New York, towards his father's house which was now his own, and bowed reverently.

He has exhibited all of the signs, and he is exceeding expectations.

Good work Jason! Despite acting without approval. We shall begin to prepare for MK-ULTRA. The Messiah project is reactivated.

www.ingramcontent.com/pod-product-compliance
Lightning Source LLC
Chambersburg PA
CBHW061220170626
46809CB00007B/2537